THE SOLDIER'S WOMAN

When Lieutenant Alain d'Albert was deserted by his girlfriend, a replacement was at hand in the shape of Christina Calvi, whose yearning for respectability through marriage did not quite coincide with her profession as a soldier's woman. Christina's obsessive love for Alain was not returned. The handsome hussar married an heiress and banished the soldier's woman from his life. But Christina was unswerving in the pursuit of her dream and Alain found his resistance weakening . . .

FREDA M. LONG

◆

THE SOLDIER'S WOMAN

Complete and Unabridged

LINFORD
Leicester

First published in Great Britain in 1987 by
Robert Hale Limited
London

First Linford Edition
published 1999
by arrangement with
Robert Hale Limited
London

British Library CIP Data

Long, Freda M. (Freda Margaret), *1932* –
The soldier's woman.—Large print ed.—
Linford romance library
1. Love stories
2. Large type books
I. Title
823.9'14 [F]

ISBN 0–7089–5487–1

Published by
F. A. Thorpe (Publishing) Ltd.
Anstey, Leicestershire

Set by Words & Graphics Ltd.
Anstey, Leicestershire
Printed and bound in Great Britain by
T. J. International Ltd., Padstow, Cornwall

This book is printed on acid-free paper

1

Strasbourg
July, 1805

The Café Violette was rapidly filling up with its usual complement of local tradesmen, army officers and members of the female sex. The first and second sorts were never accompanied to the café by their wives and the third sort, lacking the protection of husbands, were drawn there by the possibility of catching lovers. It was a nicely balanced social arrangement.

Three hussars, red-and white-plumed shakos tucked confidently under their arms, braided dolmans bristling with gold lace, threaded their way through the occupied tables to their favourite corner, and having deployed and secured their positions, looked about them with the air of men who have important business to transact. They were in a situation which called for amendment at the earliest available opportunity.

That very day one of their number had sustained a humiliating loss. The pretty, dark-eyed girl-friend of Lieutenant Alain d'Albert, who hailed from the cold northern shores of Brittany, had deserted him. The deceitful young person had waited until Alain had departed from his lodgings to go about his morning's business — which included nothing more arduous than watching some new recruits bungling through their cavalry drill — and had then gathered up her meagre possessions in preparation for immediate flight.

When Alain had returned home, a little before noon, not a trace of the charming creature remained. I say not a trace. There was one small and insignificant length of pink ribbon reposing on the tousled bed, a teasing twist of silk to mock the returning lover. The offending scrap had been seized upon and ground under the heel of an immaculate boot, but it refused to be annihilated and was at length cast into the fire, where it swiftly disintegrated into a small black blob.

As the realisation slowly dawned upon him that Yvonne had left without so much as a scrawled note of explanation or apology, Alain had begun to experience a mixture of emotions, among which neither sorrow nor despair held pride of place. Anger, disgust and shame chased each other, in that order, through his fevered brain, forming the notion that Yvonne had found him sexually inadequate; it was an idea scarcely to be borne.

Alain's two friends, Lieutenants Emil Durand and Nicolas Lemot, when informed of the gross act of betrayal, shared the feelings of their comrade-in-arms and were scathing in their condemnation of the absconding Bretonne. 'Ungrateful little *coquine*' was undoubtedly the most polite epithet assigned to her. Immediate action was called for and it was decided that the

Café Violette was the most obvious place in which to drown one's sorrows and to cast one's net among the female fish which swam about in that cosmopolitan establishment.

Emil deposited his shako on the floor at his feet and leant back against the dusty velveteen upholstery of the banquette. 'What we really need,' he said, baring the whitest of white teeth, 'is a new campaign, a whiff of gunpowder, the music of the trumpets signalling the charge. Nothing in this world is quite so exhilarating as a battle and nothing is better calculated to make one forget the devilish antics of women.'

The young man's dark eyes were filled with the elation of times remembered. 'What we want, my friends, is a gruelling march over the Alps, culminating in another Marengo.'

'Heaven forbid it!' The exclamation came from Nicolas, who caught the eye of a passing waiter and ordered three cognacs. 'We were fortunate to come out of that mess in one piece, or in three separate, badly soiled pieces if you want to be exact.'

'Three scarecrows,' confirmed Alain. 'My uniform was cut to ribbons. We all know, of course, that our revered Emperor was not himself that day. His first mistake was to underestimate the strength of the enemy and his second to run short of ammunition. He made more errors than a raw recruit and we owe our skins to General Desaix, who is no longer alive to dispute His Majesty's claim that it was he alone who won the day for France.'

Nicolas was shaking his head and eyeing the other two with the serious intensity of the born pedant. He said, 'While acknowledging the fact that Desaix played a vital part in securing our victory, let us not forget that the arrival of Kellermann with his cuirassiers and Marmont with his guns finally put the issue beyond doubt.'

'Is that a quote from your precious journal?' teased Emil.

Nicolas ignored him. His journal was his own affair. Could he help it if he had been born with the instincts of a recording angel?

Emil was exchanging glances with Alain. 'If you two must utter calumnies against the Emperor, do you mind keeping your voices down?' He spoke lightly, but his eyes warned the others to be on their guard. Strasbourg was alive with spies of every colour and denomination and a careless word could, at best, cost an officer his chances of promotion.

The hint was taken. 'Shall we observe the ladies?' Alain suggested amiably. A look of good humour irradiated the strong, sharply-cut features, and Emil and Nicolas, who had first been attracted by the relaxed mouth and mildly amused blue eyes, thought him a thoroughly decent and easy-going fellow.

Appearances, though, can be deceptive. Decent enough Alain d'Albert was, but behind the seemingly carefree, careless manner there lurked a steely self-assurance, a gift handed down to him by his aristocratic forebears, who had commanded absolute obedience from those of inferior degree until the Revolution had carried their descendants away on a tide of blood.

The d'Albert family had indeed been members of the old aristocracy of France, a fact which their deposed descendant was careful never to reveal to strangers in these post-revolutionary days, when the son of a pastrycook from the slums of Paris could rise to the rank of general — God preserve Pierre François Augereau and spare him for further deeds of valour. The d'Alberts, who, since the dawn of time had held their land south of the river Dordogne, in the Bordeaux region of France, were now, by the lips of their latest son, consigned to the rôle of moderately prosperous shop-keepers. The fact that d'Albert père had mounted the steps of the scaffold in the Place de la Révolution, maintaining his dignity to the last despite his torn and stained garments and his travesty of a wig, remained a closely-guarded secret, known only to those whom Alain would have trusted with his life. Numbered among the honoured were Emil Durand and Nicolas Lemot.

Alain had been thirteen years old at the time his father had made that last painful, jolting journey through the streets of Paris, an age when the full impact of such a tragedy struck him to the heart; and his adolescent imagination had embellished the scene of Claude d'Albert's last moments with horrifying details which thereafter he confronted daily through a series of mind-pictures which would not go away. Seated beside his weeping mother and his frightened, nine-year-old sister in their wretched one-room lodging in the Quai d'Anjou, Alain had waited for the fatal hour to come and go on that dismal February day in 1793 and had conjured up his own private vision of hell.

But the d'Albert family had had little time in which to indulge their grief; from the moment that the Count of Moissac's head had fallen beneath the blade of the guillotine, the struggle for survival was on. Having had the rôle of family bread-winner so unexpectedly thrust upon her, the widowed Countess shrugged off the indolence of thirty-nine years and cast about her for some means of profitable employment. The fact that she was a talented embroideress was of small account, since she was devoid of the skills of a plain sempstress. She therefore advertised herself as a teacher of music and in this new egalitarian world found herself giving piano lessons to the daughters of tradesmen, such people who, in former times, would not have dared to set foot beyond the confines of her kitchens.

Citizeness d'Albert, as she now styled herself — a title which was later changed to Madame when the fierce revolutionary wind had blown itself out — became quite successful in her new vocation. Her young pupils responded at once to an authoritarian but exquisitely courteous firmness as she passed on to them all the knowledge imparted to her, at considerable expense to her parents, by Christophe Glück, once the music-master of Queen Marie Antoinette, that poor, maligned woman so soon to share the fate of her late, lamented husband.

By dint of saving every spare *sou* of her meagre earnings — tradesmen in general were not in the habit of over-pricing the skills which they were so keen for their daughters to acquire — Madame d'Albert put aside enough money to clothe herself and her children decently, knowing that the self-respect which stemmed from a neat appearance was the first essential which must go towards recapturing something of the family's former glory. Her life now revolved around her children and the goals were clearly marked out.

For the girl, Célestine, the redemption

of a good marriage must be the first consideration; a marriage to be made in England, perhaps, where the people still loved their monarch and where a nobleman might be persuaded that a beautiful but penniless French countess would adorn the household of his second son most charmingly. But whatever came to pass Madame had no doubt at all that Célestine's face would be her fortune.

For Alain the path ahead was more easily definable. He must join the army. The path was clear, but the way was uncertain. For months Hélène d'Albert looked about her for a string to pull — how simple it would have been in the old days when strings required only the lightest of tugs! — and eventually found one in the person of Thérésia de Fontenay, a distant, pre-revolutionary acquaintance. Thérésia, a good-hearted woman, and no stranger to the inside of the dreaded Conciergerie prison, from which she had been rescued in the nick of time by her future husband, secured a place for Alain in the École Militaire of Paris. At the age of seventeen the young man passed out of the academy as a fully-fledged lieutenant and was assigned to the 7th Regiment of Hussars, garrisoned at Strasbourg.

By the time Alain had completed his twentieth year and had begun to frequent the salon of the famous Parisian hostess, Anne de Stael, he had seen service in Italy, campaigning with the brilliant young general, Napoleon Bonaparte. He had watched the small, energetic man, who could inspire one to perform deeds of sacrificial valour with a few well-chosen words, site and aim thirty pieces of artillery along the western bank of the river Lodi; and had made the famous crossing of the bridge in the wake of General Massena.

Alain's friend, Emil, had no such aristocratic past to hide, which may have accounted for his more cheerful disposition. He hailed from Gascony and was short and swarthy, with black, almond-shaped eyes and a long pointed nose which kinked at the bridge, where an Austrian sword with fell intent had connected to flesh and bone. Emil's father was a tailor in the town of Pau. Far removed from the blood-bath taking place in Paris and other large cities and towns, Gabriel Durand had toasted the death of the aristos in a fine red vintage, without quite comprehending the extent of the atrocities being carried out in the name of liberty, equality and fraternity. By the time he did, the arbitrary arrests and mockeries of trials were all past history. What had been done had been done, Gabriel would say with an expressive shrug, and then quickly pass on to the infinitely more enthralling subject of his soldier son, his brave Emil, who had already risen from the ranks to become an officer and would, without doubt, end his days as a general.

The third member of the trio, the historically-minded Nicolas, was the son of a schoolmaster and might have followed in his father's footsteps had it not been for the fact that a regiment of Chasseurs-à-Cheval broke ranks in the square of his home village of Pont de Cheruy, near Lyon, on a sweltering day in July, 1797, and falling into attitudes of total exhaustion against house walls, gazed with some degree of malice upon a group of youths — of whom Nicolas was one — who were frolicking about the village pump and exchanging playful cuffs and pleasantries. Their sergeant, despite his somewhat tarnished condition, resultant upon a march of nine hours, was not the man to waste such a God-given opportunity, and in no time at all had embarked upon an unofficial recruitment drive.

The dormant senses of the unimaginative seventeen-year-old who was Nicolas Lemot received a rude and unexpected shock, and waking with a start, succumbed without a murmur to the lure of a fancy uniform and the promise of glory. To his parents' dismay their only son enlisted on one day and departed, to the sound of fife and drum, on the next, and with scarcely a backward glance at the home of his childhood, disappeared in a cloud of dust.

Strange to relate, the unlikely, spotty-faced material which marched off to war on that steaming July day was transformed in the space of six months into a true soldier of France, fearless in battle and meticulous to a fault in the performance of his duty. At the battle of Marengo on 14 June, 1800, Nicolas Lemot fought with such bravery and disregard for his own safety under the very nose of his commanding officer, that the withholding of a commission would have seemed churlish. The new lieutenant was instantly transferred to the 7th Hussars, who had suffered heavy losses in the bloody engagement.

Three pairs of eyes subjected the ladies of the Café Violette to an intense and careful scrutiny, a process which continued for upwards of twenty minutes while nine cognacs were consumed. The business in hand, which was to find a replacement for the errant Yvonne, was of a serious nature and was not to be conducted lightly. A soldier's woman was a different thing altogether from your common or garden whore and must be chosen not only for her beauty, but for her neatness of attire, the details of her toilette and for her general air of being a cut above her money-grubbing sisters.

Once having accepted the protection of a particular officer a good soldier's woman was wont to display all the fidelity and obedience of a wife, cooking for, cleaning for, and nursing her man through sickness and wounding for as long as the arrangement was pleasing to both parties. Some had even been known to form incredibly durable relationships, lasting through several years of campaigning, but this was rare. Snobbish in their own way, the young women were always on the look-out for 'promotion' in their somewhat precarious careers, and it was not uncommon for a handsome captain to be ditched in favour of a broken and battle-scarred colonel. If a soldier's woman looked to the future at all, it was to the day when she might become the proprietress of a modest *pension* in a garrison town, maintaining a single state in preference to making an inferior marriage.

It was Emil who broke the protracted silence by addressing Alain. 'I think I see something which might suit you down to the ground, my friend.' The slow smile which accompanied these words suggested a *coup de maître*. 'The lady is dark and unusually beautiful for one of her kind.'

Alain's interest was instantly awakened. 'Where? Where is this paragon?'

'Turn your head a little to the left.'

Alain did so and a moment later uttered a small sound of disbelief. 'You cannot mean the one in the blue dress with the flowers in her hair?'

'The very same.'

A shake of the head denied the

possibility that the girl in the blue dress could be considered as a candidate for protection. 'That one looks far too respectable. She has an air of breeding.'

'Respectable, well-bred girls do not come to the Café Violette without a chaperone,' countered Emil.

'Ask her to dance,' suggested Nicolas. 'A few minutes of conversation will settle all.'

Still hesitant, Alain turned again to look at the girl and saw at once that he had become an object of interest. He even thought he detected a hint of challenge in her frank, openly appraising stare, and his response to this was automatic. To the accompaniment of muted murmurs of encouragement from his friends, he eased himself out from behind the table.

The girl in the blue dress received the slight bow of the handsome lieutenant with unaffected pleasure, smiling up at him and greeting him without any trace of that coyness which seemed to be the stock-in-trade of young ladies on the catch for a husband. The straightforward approach was reassuring and confirmed her status.

'Good-evening, Lieutenant.' She might have been in a Paris salon, welcoming a well-known friend.

'Will you permit me?' He indicated a vacant chair at her table. 'I hope my presence is welcome to you?'

'Very welcome.' A slight, graceful gesture of the hand gave consent.

At close quarters, and judging her by his own standards, she was not quite as beautiful as Emil had proclaimed her. Lustrous brown hair, modishly styled, and a near-flawless complexion were not matched by symmetry of feature. A blade-sharp nose, set in the triangular face, did not balance the large mouth, which turned down slightly at the corners; intelligent blue eyes surveyed Alain from beneath a high, sloping forehead, the brow of an intellectual. Taken as a whole, her face suggested a kind of spiritual avariciousness, a lust to possess the minds and hearts of those for whom she formed an attachment.

Alain, searching only for temporary sexual solace and comfortable companionship, saw nothing more beyond the veiled region of the attentive eyes than a desire similar to his own. Years of soldiering and masculine company had slightly blunted sensitivity and his one-time impeccable salon deportment was frayed round the edges.

'Are you looking for a protector?'

The warm smile was replaced by an expression of elegant distaste. 'Ah, you French, you are always so direct.'

He felt embarrassed and feigned surprise. 'You are not . . . ?' He was going to say, 'in want of a protector?' but she chose to misunderstand him.

'French? No, I was born near Turin, of an Italian father and an Austrian mother, which makes one half of me France's bitter enemy.'

'Does that half include your heart?'

Her look was steady and serious. 'No, my heart is engaged with France. Only my head, which is unequivocally Austrian, tells me that we got the worst of the bargain at Campo Formio and shall continue to get the worst of any bargain proposed by Napoleon Bonaparte until he is on the losing side.'

It was not a very astute remark, but it did astonish him beyond measure. Instead of trying to impress him with her desirability as a woman, this girl was dabbling in politics and controversy and expressing her opinions in faultless French. He was tempted to laugh, but formed the impression that had he done so she would have got up and walked away. The small choking sound which rose in his throat was covered with a cough.

'What is your name?'

The blue eyes openly mocked him. 'Your face tells me that you do not think war and politics are suitable subjects for the weaker sex.'

Irritation added an edge to his voice. 'Most women understand little of either. Regrettably, that does not seem to stop them from babbling all kinds of foolishness and pronouncing judgments which have been formed on no greater authority than the editor of a cheap newspaper or journal.'

She had put him on the defensive and something prompted him to add, 'The Emperor has freed the Italian people from the Austrian yoke. Think of the advantages they have gained from the operation of his Civil Code.'

Her smile told him that she was claiming a minor victory. 'The Italian half of me is truly grateful. Do you still want to know my name?'

'Tell me.'

'It is Christina Calvi.'

'And mine is Alain d'Albert.'

'Do you still want to come to an arrangement with me?'

For some unaccountable reason Alain felt himself blushing. 'Perhaps not.'

She continued to regard him with that same lively and challenging look, showing neither surprise nor disappointment, and he fancied that his cheeks were growing warmer by the second. He wanted more than anything to get up without vouchsafing another word and beat a retreat, but then he would have felt that she had put him to the rout and such a humiliation would be intolerable.

His next words came out in a rush. 'I beg your pardon if I have offended you. My reluctance is occasioned by the fact that you look to me more like a respectable young lady in search of a husband rather than a demi-whore who is anxious to come to an arrangement with a soldier of France.'

Her laughter bubbled over. 'Oh, Lieutenant, I like that . . . a demi-whore. You have an amusing way of expressing yourself.'

When she laughed she threw back her head in what seemed to him a completely natural manner, or was she being deliberately flirtatious? The smoothness of her throat tempted his fingers and a small frown of puzzlement dented his forehead.

'How *did* you come to be here? What of your family?'

'My mother and father died of the plague which swept through Turin and its surrounding villages last year. I have no brothers or sisters.'

The statement sounded flat and unregretful and Alain was left with the feeling that the sad event had created no emotional scars. Not every child loves its parents. Words of sympathy would have seemed inappropriate and he said nothing before she went on, 'I came into a little money from the sale of my parents' effects and decided to travel with the army. There was a girl whom I knew in Turin who had done the same thing. She told me that she had stayed in every garrison town in France before she married a sergeant in the 4th Demi-Brigade Légère. He was wounded at

Marengo and they came back to live in Turin.'

'And is it your ambition to marry a sergeant?'

Sensing a vein of amusement running through his question she did not reply to it directly. 'It was a good enough match for the daughter of a blacksmith.'

Curiosity got the better of him. 'What was your father's occupation?'

A slight hesitation preceded her answer, so slight as to pass unnoticed. 'He was a public official. His work had to do with enforcing the law.'

'Oh, a servant of the state.'

'Yes, *un fonctionnaire*.' She took hold of a gold locket which hung by a chain about her neck and snapped it open. 'This is my mother.'

He leaned forward to inspect the miniature and smiled approvingly at the portrait of a fair-haired, grey-eyed woman. 'She was very beautiful.' Something in her expression forced a second observation. 'If we two were to form a relationship I could not offer you marriage. If the enemies of France do not finish me off on the battlefield, I shall one day resign my commission and return to Paris to look after my sister and my widowed mother.'

She digested this information in silence, regarding him with the fixed gaze of a child who is doing its best to understand what is being said. He realised, long afterwards, that it was this very air of childlike innocence, combined with the audacity of her decision to 'follow the army,' as she put it, which added to the attraction he had begun to feel towards her somewhat eccentric style of beauty.

She tilted her head to one side and said with the nearest approach to coyness which she had yet displayed, 'Do you want to look after me, Alain?'

'I think we might give the arrangement a try,' came the cautious response.

From across the crowded room two congratulatory grins were directed at Alain, his friends having already anticipated his success. The German band struck up and the Café Violette was filled with the slow, sweet strains of a minuet.

2

Strasbourg
July – August, 1805

Alain was only slightly astonished to discover that Christina was a virgin and that he had, so to speak, inaugurated her career as a soldier's woman. She quickly learned the arts and artifices of love, and since Alain was a fairly demanding lover, soon became proficient in catering for his every need. The word proficient may seem an odd one to apply to haphazard bedroom activities, too sterile by half, but in Christina's case it was appropriate enough; she brought to love-making all the keen application of a dedicated apprentice whose indentures have only a month to run. Alain was both pleased and amused by her desire to do well in her new trade and warmly approved her method of 'keeping house.'

The young lieutenant rented two rooms on the top floor of a pink-stuccoed house fronting the cathedral square in the old part of the town. The house, owned by a formidable lady who rejoiced in the name of Madame La Harpe, was situated directly opposite the west door of the cathedral itself, affording a view of the elaborate façade, with its abundance of human and animal figures carved out of the sandstone and condemned to perpetual indulgence in a variety of frenzied activities, most of which were not without sin. Their living counterparts, the jugglers, acrobats and sword-swallowers who entertained the public in the square seemed less animated by comparison, so cunningly had the sculptors exercised their craft.

In a matter of days Alain's drab rooms underwent a pleasing transformation as untidy outposts of masculine and military paraphernalia were neatly stored away in cupboards and drawers. Bowls of pot-pourri and nosegays of flowers, artistically arranged in glass jars, added the final touch. As a reward for her labours, and because it amused him to do so, Alain taught Christina to fence, using two blunted weapons for the purpose.

Emil was frankly envious of his friend. 'You should have my Elise,' he complained, without losing his cheerful smile, 'a volcano in bed, but out of it the most disorganised slut in Strasbourg. She cannot even prepare the breakfast without spilling coffee beans all over the place and my room looks a mess. I tell you, Alain, my friend, you are the luckiest man in the regiment.'

Alain's smile was maddeningly fatuous. 'You should train your *mignonne*,' he admonished Emil, 'and teach her to be a good little campaign wife.'

It was not long before the young men of the 7th Hussars had more to think about than the merits or deficiencies of their girls. The Emperor was planning a new campaign. The Peace of Amiens, concluded in March, 1802 between England and France, would have been more aptly named the Truce of Amiens. Certainly First Consul Bonaparte, as he then was, had regarded the ensuing period as nothing more than a respite in which to expand his lungs and to tighten his grip on his conquests, against the day when fresh fields would open up before him and he would once more march with his troops. The dream that he would eventually conquer the world seemed infinitely believable.

By May, 1803 the treaty signed at Amiens was a dead letter and the Emperor had added Switzerland and more of Italy to his possessions. England's declaration of war was received almost with pleasure and while French troops began massing at Boulogne and at other towns along the Channel coast, a strengthened French navy was despatched to Martinique to bombard English ports, in the hope that

31

at least part of the English fleet would be drawn away to follow them. Having lured the enemy's navy half across the world the French fleet would then turn tail and make for the English Channel to support their Emperor's invasion of that land of shopkeepers whom he held in such contempt.

But the Emperor had reckoned without Admiral Lord Nelson. Chase the French he did and brought them swiftly to battle off the coast of Spain, near Cape Trafalgar. They and their Spanish allies were long to remember the Englishman's tactics as he sliced through their battle-lines and picked them off one by one.

It may be that Napoleon, deep down in his soul, had known how it would be. Two months before the battle of Trafalgar took place he had withdrawn all his troops from the Channel coast and had marched them across Europe towards Vienna, which he captured on 13 November. When he learned of Admiral Villeneuve's crushing defeat at Trafalgar he muttered crossly, 'I cannot be everywhere at once.'

The 7th Hussars received instructions to join the Emperor's army at Ettingen on 2 October. On the eve of the regiment's departure Christina flung her arms round Alain's neck and murmured into his ear, 'Do not go to the war, Alain. Tell your colonel that you are sick.'

Alain opened his mouth and roared with laughter, his breath ruffling the curls on her forehead. She drew back from him, pouting. 'You do not have to help Bonaparte fight all his battles, do you?' and before he could answer, 'What is he going to do, this famous emperor-general, when he has used up all the young men in France?'

He disengaged himself from her clinging arms and rose from the table where he had been enjoying the veal escalope which she had carefully prepared for him. His laughter had subsided and his expression had changed to one of mild concentration.

'Bring me my sabre.'

She did so, while he took possession of the only upholstered chair which the room boasted, shooting out his booted legs in the indolent attitude of a cavalryman at ease. The sabre lay across his knees, the deadly shining blade hidden inside a scabbard of embossed leather. Wearing its false colours, the death-dealing weapon was merely a pleasingly decorative accessory to the uniform of a hussar.

Alain glanced up at Christina, who was hovering over him with a worried, maternal look, so much at variance with her eighteen years. 'You must not speak so disrespectfully of the Emperor, my little Austrian traitor.'

'I hate him!' She stamped her foot to emphasize her opinion, a small, petulant slap of her leather slipper against the wooden floor. 'He never stops making war on people. Why cannot he be content with what he has gained and live in peace with his neighbours?'

An exclamation of impatience escaped him. 'What nonsense you talk. No one is more devoted to the concept of maintaining peace in Europe than the Emperor. If you are looking for somewhere to lay the blame for keeping the war on the boil, why not choose the shoulders of the King of England and the Emperors of Austria and Russia, all of whom sign friendship treaties with France with one hand and deeds of coalition against the Emperor with the other?'

Christina was gathering up the dirty crockery from the table. Over her shoulder she said, 'Perhaps they do not fully appreciate the necessity of Bonaparte's grand design, which I suppose is to rearrange all the frontiers of Europe to his own satisfaction.'

'Enough!' he roared, his anger fired by her shrewd assessment of the Emperor's aspirations. 'I cannot stand the way your tongue meddles with affairs which you do not understand. It is so . . . so . . . ' — he groped for the right word and came up with one of his mother's favourite descriptions for a bold woman — 'You have an indelicate tongue. If we are to stay together you must stop acting like that particularly nasty breed who call themselves political journalists.'

The remark provoked a reaction which he had not anticipated. Abandoning her task at the table, Christina came to kneel at his feet and placing both her hands on the sabre lying crosswise before her, said pleadingly, 'Alain, please, do not be angry with me. I could not bear it if you were to tell me to go. Oh, my darling, you must know by now that I adore you.'

'Come now, do not be so foolish.' He sounded uncomfortable. 'You know that our arrangement is only temporary. You must not make such extravagant statements.'

Quite gently he removed her hands from his knees and grasping the hilt of the sabre, withdrew it from the scabbard. The stealthy, whispering sound of steel against leather made her shiver with distaste. He pretended not to notice the quick intake of breath as he ran his thumb along the edge of the weapon, testing the blade for keenness.

Curiosity overcame the repugnance she always felt at the sight of the unsheathed sabre. 'How do you kill a man with that?'

His face altered slightly, reflecting a faint unease that a woman should pose such a question. 'You cannot really want to know.'

'I do. Indeed, I do,' she insisted earnestly. 'I want to know how you earn your soldier's pay.'

His mouth tightened. 'Well then, one tries to take off the head of one's enemy with a single cut, but the attempt is rarely successful. More often than not one must rest content with cutting the other fellow's throat, or slicing off his ear. The action of one's horse, you see, precludes perfect accuracy.

'On the other hand, it is not unknown for a cannon ball to take off a head. I once saw an Austrian dragoon, minus his head, ride past me still maintaining an upright posture in the saddle. I remember wondering at the time if the poor bastard would have two graves, one for his head and another for his body. Queer thoughts like that often run through my head in the heat of battle.'

She held his gaze while he continued speaking, then lowered her head to whisper, 'War is so cruel. You are cruel too, Alain. You say these things to punish me and make me feel miserable.'

'You punish yourself,' he riposted, 'by wanting to know things it is better for you not to know.'

She raised serious and troubled eyes to meet his. 'I wish I could put on a uniform and come with you. I wish I could ride by your side against the enemy, then I should not have to wait here, week after week, hearing nothing of you, knowing nothing, and all the time wondering if you are ever coming back to me.'

Emil had described Christina as being unusually beautiful. Looking at her now, in her mood of anxious despair, Alain knew what his friend had meant. Her features certainly did not conform to the conventional pattern of beauty, but there were moments when her expression transformed the ordinary into the extraordinary, and this was one of them.

A brief, unaccustomed tenderness welled up in the breast of Alain d'Albert for this girl who shared his life. He said, 'I am truly flattered by your concern for my hide, but you must not try to divert me from my duty.'

Still on her knees before him, she leaned forward and ran a tentative forefinger down the entire length of the sabre. 'Have you had this blessed by the priest?'

He looked startled. 'Certainly not. I leave all that kind of superstitious rubbish to those who are afraid to die.'

'Are not you afraid to die, Alain?'

'I never think about it,' he replied truthfully. 'I go into battle to do a job and to earn my soldier's pay, as you put it.'

She gave a small, defeated sigh. 'While you are away I shall pray for you every day.'

'I cannot stop you.'

'Alain!'

Her voice rose to a wail which clawed at his already overstretched nerves — a battle in prospect invariably wound him up to a feverish pitch of excitement — and stirred him again to anger. 'For God's sake, Christina, do not ask of me more than I have the capacity to give. Stop suffocating me with your self-induced anguish.'

He grabbed her by the shoulders and pushed her away from him so that she almost fell backwards. With a struggle she recovered herself and burst into tears, sinking to the floor and burying her face in her hands. His thoughts returned with longing to the days when the gay, uncomplicated Yvonne had lifted his spirits with her amusing, inconsequential chatter, and had then abandoned him without so much as a few light-hearted words of apology.

Imagination conjured up what she might have said to him had she bothered to put pen to paper: 'My dear Alain, you do understand that I simply cannot afford to miss an opportunity like this? There is a certain colonel who . . . ' Yvonne had angered him with her wordless flight, but perhaps hers had been the better way . . . a clean break without fuss.

Alain vacated his chair and went to stand over the huddled figure, addressing it in terms of uncompromising firmness. 'When I leave here tomorrow, I have no way of knowing whether my return will be delayed by weeks, months or even beyond a year. I may never return if my previous good fortune deserts me. These lodgings are paid for until Christmas, after which time you must vacate them, unless you can find someone else who is willing to come and live here and be your protector.'

Ignoring her gasp of protest he went on, still in that slightly hectoring tone, 'Christina, I do not wish you to wait for me. You say you are in love with me and I am sorry for it. I did not set out to capture your heart, nor did I anticipate that such a thing would happen without some effort on my part, and I hope you give me credit for not being the sort of man who would stoop to trifle with the affections of another without thought of the pain which that might cause.'

She had stopped crying but remained perfectly still, taut and tensely listening, like an animal which fears the attack of the predator and curls itself into a ball in the hope that it will be overlooked. It irritated him to see her so; he reached down to pull her to her feet, but she fended him off with her arm. Shrugging, he turned away and strode towards the door.

'Where are you going?'

'To see Emil and Nicolas. There are certain arrangements to be made before our departure tomorrow.'

'You will come back . . . so that we can spend this last night together?'

The distressed child was begging him for one last small favour. 'Yes,' he replied wearily, 'I promise to come back.'

3

Austerlitz
December, 1805

The autumn of 1805 was exceptionally cold and rain dropped incessantly from a full-bellied sky. The men of the 7th Hussars, along with every other man of every other regiment in the French army, talked of nothing but the weather and became boringly repetitious about damp clothes, waterlogged boots and pistols which would not fire.

Alain, Emil and Nicolas did their fair share of grumbling and their fair share of fighting, trailing across eastern Europe in the wake of the Emperor, who brought the Austrians and the Prussians to battle whenever a favourable opportunity occurred. In November they fought at Hollabrünn and at Wischau, mere preliminary skirmishes before the grand massacre which they knew was to come.

On 28 November the Emperor's *Grande Armée* arrived at Brunn in Moldavia and moving on a few kilometres to the east of the town, camped out on frost-hardened ground. The combined armies of Russia, Prussia and Austria, eighty-nine thousand strong, awaited the pleasure of the Emperor of France at Olmutz, which lay about fifty kilometres to the north of the village of Austerlitz. The Emperor, wily as a fox, feigned weakness and led his enemies on to the killing ground.

The battle which began at nine o'clock on the morning of 2 December, 1805 was the fiercest engagement in which Alain had ever taken part. The 7th Hussars formed part of Marshal Murat's massed cavalry divisions, their task on this fateful day to hurl themselves against the squadrons of the Prince of Liechtenstein, deployed in the open plain below the Pratzen Heights.

At three o'clock in the afternoon

Alain, flanked by Emil and Nicolas, deployed in echelon in preparation for his fifth cavalry charge of the day. With some reluctance he had changed horses and had left his favourite mount, Roland, in the picket lines; a deep gash above the withers had earned the animal his respite. Alain, for whom no respite was possible, had resolutely dismissed the tiny worm of suspicion which nagged at his exhausted brain and bred superstition. Would a change of horses change his luck? Would a fifth cavalry charge prove to be one too many for Alain d'Albert?

'Liechtenstein's left has been routed!' Emil shouted above the tumult of neighing horses and intermittent artillery fire. 'One more hearty blow and we shall have them!' The news, which had been transmitted along the line with the speed of a flame along a trail of gunpowder, lifted Alain's spirits. He passed it on to Nicolas, who smiled his sober smile and calmly caressed his horse's neck.

Alain waited impatiently now for the trumpeters to signal the charge, raising his sabre to his lips in the customary gesture of salutation to the unseen gods of battle. The red and sinking sun was reflected in a sweep of curved steel as he lowered the weapon and gathered the reins of his horse in his left hand. The chestnut stallion, an unknown quantity upon whose performance his rider's life might depend, was fresh and eager to be off. Alain patted his neck and wished him good fortune. '*Bonne chance, mon cousin.*'

He stood up in the saddle, straining his eyes against the lowering sun. On either side of him Emil and Nicolas were doing the same. The signal came, a series of eight, brass-tongued notes, repeated over and over again, and they were off, opening their throats to let forth the orchestrated savagery of defiance against the enemy, which served at the same time as a spur to endeavour and a barrier against gut-churning fear. The steady beat of the horses' hooves provided a muted counterpoint to the harsh, discordant shouts of men charging to death or glory.

In a blink of time as it seemed to Alain, he was upon the enemy and staring into the mustachioed face of an Austrian dragoon whose menacing aspect provoked only scorn, as did the braggadocio tugging at his mount's bit to make the animal rear and paw the air. It was this clownish, undisciplined display which almost proved to be Alain's undoing, for it momentarily distracted him from his purpose, which was to despatch his opponent in the shortest possible time. His sabre slashed downwards seconds after the Austrian's weapon sliced through the epaulette on his right shoulder and bit into his upper arm. Even as he recoiled, the Austrian withdrew the embedded blade of his sabre and thundered past the stricken hussar to engage his next victim.

A flooding warmth spreading down his arm told Alain that his wound was deep. In the circumstances to have engaged another of the enemy would have been foolish bravado; the Emperor was winning his battle and had no need of empty heroes. Alain spurred his horse forward, parried a weak thrust from a passing Russian dragoon, whose face was a mask of blood, and cantered through the thinning lines. Veering to the left he made for the neutrality of a hazel copse where other wounded men had taken refuge. As he rode away from the scene of carnage he glanced over his shoulder, striving to catch a glimpse of Emil and Nicolas, but if his friends were among the flailing, twisting contestants still hammering it out on the field, it would have been impossible to distinguish them from all those other grotesquely contorted figures struggling to survive.

Once having gained the shelter of the copse, Alain did not dismount, but pressed on in a westerly direction towards the field hospital. He was conscious of the fact that he was losing a great deal of blood and that if his wound was not soon staunched by professional hands he might yet die. Waves of nausea washed over him and a deadly faintness blotted out the sights and sounds of the waning afternoon. His head lolled on his breast and the reins slid through his slackening grip. His sabre, which he prized beyond any of his other few possessions, dropped, point downwards, into the soggy ground and disappeared for ever among the spoils of war. The stallion ambled on, unfettered by Alain's guiding hand, but with that marvellous, unfathomable instinct of his kind, found his way to the source of help.

The next thing Alain knew as he fought his way back to consciousness from the depths of a turbulent, heaving sea, was that an arm had encircled his waist and that he was being pulled from his horse like a sack of flour. The deep, confident tones of a sergeant of grenadiers sounded in his ears. 'Come along, Lieutenant. Easy now . . . one foot in front of the other, if you please, sir. Damn me if you are not trying to go sideways . . . there, now.'

Alain was eased down on to a board supported by trestles and felt his legs being lifted into position. Another pair of hands began busying themselves with the cutting away of his uniform jacket, and a sudden searing pain which ripped through his right shoulder and arm brought him back to a full awareness of his surroundings.

'What the devil . . . ?' He endeavoured, unsuccessfully, to twist away from the source of the pain. The flat, unemotional voice of Pasiello, the regimental surgeon, bade him be still and then, from long established habit, began a running commentary upon his work.

'We shall have this jacket off in a trice . . . bite on your fist, Lieutenant, there's a good fellow, and praise God that you will live to fight another day . . . at least, I think you will . . . one can never be sure until all is revealed. There . . . now we have it . . . one last pull . . . ah, yes, that did make you jump about a bit . . . not surprising . . . and what have we here?'

Alain, pale as a ghost from Pasiello's attentions, stifled a scream and tried to maintain some semblance of dignity commensurate with his rank, while the latter diagnosed and offered his prognosis.

'Luckily for you, Lieutenant, your opponent missed his mark . . . a touch higher and he would have opened up your jugular vein. As it is, the Emperor may rely upon you for at least one more charge the next time that damned Austrian Emperor breaks his word.'

Alain stumbled away from Pasiello's painful ministrations and his even more painful pleasantries, and pushing his way through a sea of closely-packed stretchers of groaning men, forbore to lock glances with a beseeching eye, or to notice a hand stretched towards him in silent supplication. One hand, however, was more insistent than the rest. It clutched at his leg and refused to let go.

Alain's reluctant gaze travelled downwards and encountered a well-known visage. 'Nicolas!'

Slowly, he sank to his knees beside a man who had been his constant companion for eight years. 'Jesus have mercy,' he murmured and crossed himself. The sudden reversion to the faith of his childhood would have startled him at any other time. He asked apprehensively, 'Are you badly cut up, old fellow?'

The whispered reply was barely audible. 'More full of . . . holes . . . than a sieve.' Nicolas struggled for greater coherence. 'My parents at Pont de Cheruy . . . near Lyon. Will you go to see them? Take them my things? Comfort them a little, Alain? There is some money. I want them to have it . . . and my journal. Do not forget . . . journal . . . important historical document . . . '

The effort had been too much. Nicolas closed his eyes, gave a sigh strongly reminiscent of the sound a baby makes when play has exhausted him, and left Alain to face the world with but one friend worthy of the name.

4

Strasbourg
New Year, 1806

The trauma of Austerlitz and the death of Nicolas had left Alain mentally drained. In fulfilment of his promise to his dead friend he travelled to Lyon by the public coach, gritting his teeth against the pain of his half-healed wound as the vehicle jolted along the uneven roads. At Lyon he hired a horse and rode the five kilometres to the village of Pont de Cheruy, where he received directions to the schoolmaster's house from an old man whose eyes lit up at the sight of a hussar uniform. The old man drew a heavy sigh for his lost youth.

The Lemots were stiffly polite and showed little sign of grief at the loss of their son, who, in their opinion, had basely deserted them all those years ago. The ritual words of condolence stuck in Alain's throat. What emerged was a halting affirmation of Nicolas's heroism which was received by Monsieur Lemot with the acid comment, 'No doubt the Emperor will give us a medal by which to remember our son's heroic deeds.'

Alain found such deep-seated bitterness repellent and refusing the offer of a glass of wine, quickly took his leave. Nicolas's possessions, on being handed over, merited only a brief nod of thanks from his dry-eyed mother. Alain suspected that later Madame Lemot would pay for her implacability with a heavy burden of guilt.

He had mounted his horse and was riding away from the unhappy encounter before he realised that Nicolas's journal was still in his pocket. Having had a desire to read it himself he had kept it separate from the other parcelled-up items. His first instinct was to turn back but he hesitated, fearful that the journal, in the present mood of the Lemots, would find its way into the fire. 'Nicolas, my brave friend,' he murmured, 'you and I shall soldier on together.'

After performing his duty to his friend, Alain trailed back to Strasbourg in low spirits and with his arm and shoulder on fire. He went at once to his old place of residence and applied to his former landlady for a room in her loosely run establishment.

Madame La Harpe beamed at him from behind a pair of square-rimmed spectacles which she immediately lowered, as if in salute to one of her military gentlemen.

'Your lady is waiting for you, Monsieur.'

Alain stared at her blankly. 'My mother . . . is my mother here?'

'No, no, Monsieur!' Madame La Harpe shook with laughter, setting into motion her truly monumental breasts. 'Your *lady*. She with the wicked blue eyes.'

'Mademoiselle Calvi!' Alain exclaimed at once.

Madame La Harpe nodded vigorously, adding for good measure, 'If my daughter had eyes like that, I should beat her every day to cast out the Devil.'

Alain's arm was throbbing, as it had never ceased to do since the day his wound was inflicted. It did not help much to heap curses on the head of the pig of an Austrian who had done this to him, but he frequently did so, in terms both unequivocal and obscene. Madame La Harpe's information did not plunge him into transports of delight. The last thing he wanted was a woman in his bed and at his table. But second thoughts often suggest a glimmer of light at the end of the tunnel; a certain advantage might be gained from Christina's skill as a cook, and although he had never had occasion to put her skill as a nurse to the test, he did not doubt that it would prove to be more than adequate.

After thanking Madame La Harpe, whose all-seeing eyes had grown quite moist at the sight of his strapped-up arm, Alain climbed the three flights of stairs to his old rooms. The outer door stood ajar and the suspicion that Christina had spied him from the window coming across the square was confirmed immediately he stepped across the threshold. She was standing facing him with the trembling intensity of a cat at a mouse-hole.

'Alain!' She ran towards him and would almost certainly have embraced him had he not turned quickly aside to avoid her outstretched arms and occupied the nearest chair. His refusal to demonstrate his pleasure at their reunion drained all the eagerness out of her as she hovered uncertainly before him, stating the obvious.

'You are wounded.'

'Nicolas is dead.'

'Oh . . . I am sorry.'

'Give me leave to doubt that. You never liked him.'

She lowered her eyes lest he should see the truth of his assertion written in their expression. 'Nicolas and Emil used to tease me,' she defended herself. 'They said that I behaved towards you like a wife . . . a *weibchen*. They said I should try to be more like their girls.' Her thin nose wrinkled in distaste. 'Those *coquines*, they think only of having a good time and of how many *cadeaux* they can squeeze out of their men. That slut Babette did not love Nicolas.'

'She loved him . . . in her own way. Not everyone shares your high-minded notions of the holiness of the grand passion. Have you ever stopped to think that there is something out of tune about your feelings towards me, an inappropriate possessiveness, to which I am not able to respond? It was the cause of our quarrel, if you remember, so do not, I beg you, make the same mistake again or we shall part as we did before.'

'You are not wearing your sabre.

What has become of it?'

The abrupt change of subject was typical of her reaction to his refusal to admit to any emotional involvement between them. All the same, he was glad of the diversion because his tired mind was not presently equipped to deal with Christina's bickerings.

'I dropped it somewhere in eastern Europe. It is probably now in the possession of an anonymous, looting peasant, one of those vultures who flap about battlefields when the fighting is over, gathering up everything their bloodstained beaks can find. Perhaps it will be sold to an Austrian, who will use it to kill Frenchmen. There is something for your busy brain to ponder upon. Tomorrow I shall go out and buy a new one. Today, all I want to do is to eat and sleep.'

In no time at all Alain and Christina had resumed their old, oddly domestic relationship, the former basking in the luxury of being cared for, the latter content with her new rôle of ministering angel. It was soothing for Alain to have his wound dressed by considerate and less brusquely efficient hands than those of a medical orderly. Under Christina's ministrations he relaxed and his tensions fell away. They made love frequently, like any other couple who have been reunited after a lengthy period of separation.

A few weeks after his return Alain applied to his colonel for leave. His application was successful and one evening he announced to Christina his intention of travelling to Paris to see his mother and sister.

'May I come with you?'

The request both shocked and irritated Alain. 'Certainly not. I am surprised that you should even bother to ask such a question.'

'Madame d'Albert would not approve of me,' she said in a small voice.

A thoughtless disregard for her feelings lay behind his answer. 'Whether or not my mother would approve of you is of no particular consequence, since she would not be able to receive you.'

'Because I am a whore?'

Alain was instantly moved to anger. 'What is this? Is it an exercise in self-flagellation? If so, it proves my theory that nuns and whores are sisters under the skin.'

'Sometimes I almost hate you.'

'Before I went away you said you adored me.'

'You were kinder to me then.'

'And now I am being unkind because I will not take you to see my mother?'

His words hung between them in the uneasy silence. She pressed her lips together, as if imprisoning the utterances she might later regret. He said, 'You chose your way of life, Christina. If now you are hankering after respectability you should emulate your friend by marrying a sergeant and going back to Turin.'

Her quiescent misery vanished in a moment and she was all sound and fury. 'She was not my friend! I am not like her!'

'Now we are in agreement. Your friend knew her place in the scheme of things and unless you are willing to accept the fact that *your* place is to be a soldier's woman, and nothing more, I fear we must part company.'

He had reduced her to tears, but the sight of a lachrymose female had never touched a chord of sympathy in his breast and he said impatiently, 'I shall never marry you, Christina. In your heart you must know that, you must believe that.'

Even as he spoke Alain realised that he could never make Christina believe that which her innate stubbornness denied. He gave a small sigh which spoke both defeat and exasperation. Perhaps when he returned from Paris he would tell her to go. He did not love her and it was time to declare that this was so.

'I do not love you . . . and even if I did the thing would be impossible. When I marry . . . *if* I marry, it must be with a woman who can bring me a fortune of at least fifty thousand francs a year. I shall need to buy a house and farm some land. I shall want to keep my own carriage and carriage-horses, and I shall want to go hunting, a sport which will require the acquisition of yet more horses. It is my ambition to do so many things when I resign my commission and retire from the army. Not least among them is to provide a good home for my mother and to arrange a good match for my sister, who must be generously dowered.'

She was staring at him in a thoughtful, concentrated way, as if seeking to strip away the barriers which prevented her from peering into his very soul. 'This woman who will buy you for her husband because she is too ugly to attach to herself a man of substance . . . will you tell her about me?'

They were sitting by the window, catching the last of the evening light, she with a book of fashion engravings open on her lap which she glanced at from time to time, idly turning the pages; he was content merely to stare out of the window at the almost deserted square. He felt nothing but mild amusement at her attempt to hurt his pride and focussed his attention on the lamp-lighter, who was going about his business in the square below in his usual leisurely fashion, dogged by three inquisitive small boys.

'If you are trying to make me angry I would advise you to save your breath.'

'No, really,' she protested. 'I should like to know.'

'Then the answer must be that, in my opinion, a man would be a fool to reveal all of his past to a woman whom he loves and intends to marry.'

'I am surprised that you mention love. Surely love cannot figure very largely in any contract you are likely to make. As to it being foolish in a man to reveal his past to his future wife, I cannot agree with you there. In general, I think that women are pleased to know that their chosen spouses have indulged in wild excesses. It makes them feel superior and virtuous to have captured such a rake.'

'You have no very high opinion of your own sex, I perceive.'

'On the contrary, I have the highest regard for the exclusively feminine capacity for fidelity.'

That made him laugh. 'Do you really believe that men are invariably the betrayers and women the betrayed? How little you know of the world. Even the Empress Josephine was unfaithful to her husband . . . before he became Emperor, of course, which only goes to prove that women, while having little natural inclination towards fidelity, have the greatest capacity for caution, a formidable combination of characteristics against which a mere male does not stand a chance.'

Under this bombardment of sarcasm she abandoned her line of argument and made pretence of studying her book with a deeper interest; one hand toyed with the locket which contained the miniature of her mother. That she was preparing fresh verbal torments for him he did not doubt, but in spite of his awareness of her mood her next words caught him off guard.

'You never take me to the opera or to the theatre. Are you ashamed to be seen with me?'

The lamp-lighter was attending to the light which was stationed outside the Pharmacie Cerf, hauling on the rope to lower the glass lantern, while the children watched in muted admiration as he pursued his fascinating occupation.

Alain turned his head away from the window to reply in measured tones, 'No, I am not ashamed to be seen with you, Christina, but if we were to meet, say, the wife of my colonel, who knows I am unattached, she would be forced to cut you dead, and it would grieve me to see you suffer embarrassment.'

She appeared to consider this. 'You could present me as your cousin. Neither my dress nor my deportment distinguish me as a whore, do they?'

He was determined not to lose

68

his temper with her. 'That might create difficulties during the course of conversation. For instance, if Madame Varesne were to put a question to you which concerned my family, an enquiry, perhaps, as to the exact relationship in which you and I stand, you might say something which she knew to be untrue. You would certainly be put to the expedient of telling a falsehood.'

'You assume too much,' she argued. 'Family matters are hardly likely to be discussed during a brief encounter at the opera. Polite exchanges are more the thing, and I am quite equal to those.'

He gave a light, dismissive shrug and resumed his observation of the scene below which consisted of nothing more exciting than a well-lit, empty square. There was not a single passer-by to create an interest.

The silence between them lengthened, but it was a silence filled with imagined grievances on her side. Unable at last to contain herself, she burst forth with,

'I have come to the conclusion that I chose the wrong way of life. If I had decided to marry in my station I would have been bound to my husband for the rest of my days and he to me, with all the comfort and security which that condition brings. On the other hand, if I had decided to become a whore, at least I would have been paid for my trouble. As things stand, I am neither one thing nor the other.'

'Then change your way of life and become one thing or the other,' came the testy reply, 'and before you lose your temper with me completely, I must warn you that if you say one more word our liaison will be at an end. This whole conversation stemmed from the possibility that I might marry at some future, unspecified date, an event with which you can have nothing to do.'

5

Paris
March, 1806

Paris was teeming with military men
and dispossessed aristocrats. The latter,
turned out of doors during the
Revolution, rented old and run-down
houses in Montmartre and devised ways
and means by which to exist from day
to day. Some even dreamt of recouping
their lost fortunes.

Alain hired a calèche to take him to
his mother's house in the Quai de la
Tournelle, an undistinguished, white-
stuccoed edifice facing the river which
Madame d'Albert had exchanged for
her dismal room in the Quai d'Anjou
soon after her son was commissioned.
Alain's generosity had provided the
means by which an increased rent
for the modest establishment could

be afforded; every month he sent his mother half his lieutenant's pay of one hundred and twenty livres.

Madame's circumstances had changed in one other respect. When First Consul Bonaparte had set his foot on the topmost rung of the ladder of success and had turned himself into an emperor, one of his first acts had been to encourage the return to France from exile of the old nobility. They came, parading their ancient titles and ungratefully turning up their aristocratic noses at the parvenu Imperial family. Madame d'Albert became once more the Countess of Moissac, but her re-assumed title brought with it none of the old privileges; pupils still came to her door for their weekly music lessons. No painful feelings of hurt pride were occasioned by this fact. The Countess had come to depend on the bright, eager faces of 'her children' as she called them, to enliven the quiet, secluded days she passed in the company of her daughter.

Alain paid off the driver of the calèche and mounted the three steps to the front door of the green-shuttered house. His hand, raised to the gleaming brass knocker, was anticipated. The door opened and Célestine hurled herself at him, the pink ribbons in her dark hair dancing their own jig of elation.

'Alain! Oh, Alain, you have come at last. It has been so long since we saw you . . . and that dreadful battle . . . Maman and I read about it in the newspapers. Is your wound quite healed, my brave darling?'

Thoroughly amused by this boisterous reception, and at being called a 'brave darling,' — thank heaven Emil was not present to hear that! — Alain allowed himself to be pulled into the house and there, in the small black-and white-tiled entrance hall, stood his mother, tall, proud and indomitable, with her greying hair neatly dressed and her black gown defiantly out of fashion, open as it was in front to display a white silk petticoat with pale green sprigs.

The Countess of Moissac stepped forward to greet her son. 'Alain, my dearest boy, how happy I am to see you.'

So calm, so restrained, so soothing to his ragged nerves was that whiff of the old régime, when perfect manners counted for more than the stylish elegance of one's attire.

'*Maman*!' He embraced her and planted a firm kiss upon the powdered cheek. 'You smell of violets.'

Her smile was positively arch. 'Violets are fashionable in Paris just now.'

'Am I expected to ask why?'

For answer, the Countess tucked his arm in hers and led him towards the drawing-room, with Célestine skipping ahead to hold wide the door. 'Violets,' she explained, as her son, solicitously attended by his sister, settled himself into an armchair upholstered in pale blue silk, 'are being sold by the flowerwomen on every street corner in

Paris now that spring is here. They are made into *boutonnières* and are being bought by all those who long for the return of the Bourbons. If someone should accost you in the street, Alain, and ask if you like violets, please do not imagine for one moment that you have been approached by a madman. The phrase is simply a code for 'Do you support the return of King Louis XVIII?' ' A broad smile was directed at her fascinated listener. 'As the Count of Moissac your reply would most certainly be yes.'

'But as Lieutenant d'Albert of the 7th Regiment of Hussars and the Emperor's loyal subject, my reply would most certainly be no, *Maman*,' replied Alain severely. 'Like it or not, we cannot turn back the clock now. The Emperor has given France a fresh impetus and we must go along with the tide or perish.'

'Alain, you have become a revolutionary,' accused his mother.

'I prefer to regard myself as a realist.

Corruption was rife under the Bourbons and the men who murdered my father have been consumed in the fires of their own rhetoric.'

'Talleyrand is still with us,' retorted the Countess, tightening her lips at the thought of that arch-traitor. 'I am told that during the Terror he spent most of his time abroad on diplomatic missions, and I would hazard a guess that his loyalty to his new master is not beyond question.'

The Countess, having discharged her broadside against the one-time priest turned politician, who had risen to become Grand Chamberlain of France, now instructed Célestine to offer her brother some bread and butter and announced her intention of making tea. The ritual, which Alain remembered so well from the days of his childhood, was commenced.

'I did not know you still had the silver teapot,' he remarked with surprise.

'I was forced to keep it hidden for

several years,' replied his mother, lightly caressing the handle of the beautiful object, 'but now that Bonaparte has anointed himself with holy oil it is perfectly safe to display one's coat-of-arms.'

Célestine presented the appreciative newcomer with a small plate and a snowy napkin and offered him wafer-thin slices of bread and butter spread with honey. He smiled up at her. 'How very elegant for one who is used only to soldiers' fare.'

Her eyes sparkled. 'I assure you, my dear brother, that supper will consist of something considerably more substantial. This is just to whet your appetite for a selection of delicious dishes to come.'

'Prepared by your own hands?'

'And by those of a little girl whom we hire by the day.'

'I am sure the meal will be quite excellent and speaking of excellence, that is a very charming dress you are wearing.'

Célestine glanced down at the article in question, a creation of cream silk powdered with tiny pink rosebuds and trimmed with lace. '*Maman* made it for me.'

'*Maman*?' he queried incredulously.

'Your astonishment at my skill as a sempstress does you little credit, Alain,' interposed the Countess, hiding a smile. 'I taught myself how to sew by unpicking an old dress of my own to see how it was done. I flatter myself that the result is not unpleasing.'

'I am lost in admiration,' declared her son. His eyes returned to Célestine. 'How many hearts have you broken in your circle of acquaintance with that fetching gown?'

A deep blush dyed the girl's pale cheeks and the dark eyes distanced themselves from remembered pain. She turned to look at her mother as though for help. The Countess, who was pouring tea into gold-edged china cups, came to her rescue. 'We did make the acquaintance of a young gentleman who paid some attention to Célestine,' she said, 'but looks and an impeccable pedigree were not enough, it seemed. The de Moissac name carried little weight. The plain fact is that I was unable to provide a dowry for my daughter and this could not be overlooked.'

A heavy sigh preceded the conclusion of the sad tale. 'Unhappily, Célestine's affections became rather deeply engaged before the matter was clarified.'

'But my heart is disengaged now,' Célestine claimed brightly — and untruthfully. An awkward smile was directed at her brother. 'I have quite forgotten the gentleman.'

Célestine went back to the table with the plate of bread and butter and accepted a cup of tea from her mother which she offered to Alain. Her expression told him that the subject of the acquisitive suitor was not one which she cared to pursue.

Alain gave an inward sigh for the drawbacks of poverty and asked, 'Do you keep any company these days, *Maman*?'

'Not a great deal,' replied his mother. 'About a month ago we became acquainted with a Monsieur and Madame Cabarroques who reside in the Rue Geoffroy St. Hilaire. They have a very fine house there which once belonged to Cardinal Richelieu and employ an army of servants. Célestine met their daughter, Marie-Josèphe, at a ball held in the Cabarroques' house, to which a whole host of young people had been invited.'

The Countess went on informatively, 'Monsieur Cabarroques is the owner of a large manufactory at Rouen which produces fine confectionery. He has lately become sole purveyor to the Empress Josephine who, I am given to understand, was previously supplied with cakes and *bons-bons* by an Englishman, a Mr Dollond of Bond Street in London. As you know, after the failure of the Treaty of Amiens the Emperor placed an embargo on the importation of all English goods and the Empress was forced to do her shopping elsewhere.'

The Countess smiled knowingly. 'It is rumoured that both she and Bonaparte receive secret packages from England from time to time, which contain rose bushes from Kew Gardens for her and razors from a steel manufactory in the English Midlands for him. It seems that while despising the might of English steel on the battlefield, the Emperor will use nothing else on his whiskers.'

The Countess paused briefly before adding, 'The Cabarroques are to dine with us on Tuesday next. I think you will find them tolerably good company.'

At this point Alain thought he distinguished an exchange of glances between his mother and sister, a wordless comment which each understood. The words 'fine confectionery,' floated through his head . . . a rich purveyor of fine confectionery with a marriageable daughter? Was his mother match-making? Alain did not know if he was ready for marriage, not while the Emperor was still rampaging through Europe and changing boundaries to suit himself. One so much wanted to be a part of all that. War, despite its barbarity and the personal sorrow that it frequently engendered, was undeniably addictive.

His mother's voice cut across his thoughts. 'Tell me about Austerlitz, Alain. You wrote to me that your wound was a trifle, but I know that you have a positive gift for understatement.'

'I received a sabre-cut in my upper arm, *Maman*, which is now quite healed. The stiffness will go in a little while.'

She eyed him with fond reproach. 'So I was right. The injury was worse than you would have had us believe.'

'The wound was deep but not dangerous . . . there, will that satisfy you?'

'Satisfy? That is a strange word to use. Should it satisfy me that my son has been chopped about by an Austrian madman?'

'An Austrian dragoon who was performing his duty, *Maman*, and whose mother is probably, at this very moment, clasping him to her bosom and bemoaning the fact that a mad Frenchman tried to decapitate *her* beloved son with a sabre. And before you question me further, I will tell you three things about Austerlitz. They are that I was wounded by an Austrian dragoon, that I lost one of my dearest friends, and that I saw the Emperor of Russia sit down among his dead soldiers and weep. Please, *Maman*, let us talk of common, comfortable, everyday things.'

The Cabarroques family were delightfully open and frank and only slightly conscious of the fact that they were in the presence of three members of the *Ancien Régime*.

Monsieur Cabarroques was a large, red-faced man with bulging blue eyes and a nose of equal prominence. People often told him that he looked like the King of England, an accolade which he refuted loudly and at length, but which secretly pleased him. He took a keen interest in military matters and at dinner engaged Alain in a long and involved discussion about the recent campaign. Alain remarked jokingly that Monsieur Cabarroques seemed to know more about the logistics of war than he did, to which that gentleman replied with a sad little shake of the head, 'Ah, Lieutenant, it is pure envy which prompts me to follow the details of the war so closely. If only I were not past the age when I might embark upon a career in the army and carry a sword in defence of this great country of ours.'

Alain smiled politely. He had heard it all before from older men, many of whom seemed burdened with guilt at not having been given the opportunity to spill the blood of an enemy of France.

Madame Cabarroques, dark-haired, dark-eyed and deceptively fragile looking — the exact antithesis of her booming husband — was not in the least interested in the war. Fashions and books were her favourite subjects, and a spirited exchange concerning these two absorbing items was soon in full swing between the older ladies. The talk ebbed and flowed, while the two younger ladies met glances with smiles in a silent conspiracy which seemed to hint at feminine mysteries to be disclosed later, in some virginal and private place.

The third member of the Cabarroques family, Mademoiselle Marie-Josèphe Cabarroques, had light-brown hair which curled naturally, lavender-blue eyes and a rose-petal complexion which owed nothing to art. Alain had been immediately struck by her beauty and found he could not keep his eyes from straying ever more often in her direction. She, aware of his interest, did not preen herself under the flattering masculine attention as many young women of her age and station in life might have done, but remained calm and composed and met her admirer eye to eye with a pleasant smile.

There was nothing sickly or sentimental about Marie-Josèphe. She was a straightforward, down-to-earth sort of person, someone who refused to be intimidated by people or events. At the same time, she was kind and compassionate and sparing of her criticism of others. There were some who thought she was too good to be true and were cautious in their praise of her, but they were in the minority and consisted for the most part of young, plain-faced girls with spotty complexions.

Alain, observing Marie-Josèphe's unaffected interest in all that was being said, was suddenly glad that the old days were gone and he might address himself to the daughter of a confectioner without experiencing the least feeling of condescension. How pretty she looked in her dress of lemon-coloured silk, with its little puffed sleeves and trimmings of crisp white lace, and how elegant the cream-coloured cashmere shawl which was draped so becomingly over her shoulders. Her hair, he noticed, was dressed in an unfashionably natural style and this pleased him.

Amidst Monsieur Cabarroques's military fervour and his wife's literary fervour — Madame Cabarroques was quite an authority on English novels — Alain managed to extract from Marie-Josèphe the information that she was fond of visiting picture galleries, whereupon an expedition to the Louvre palace, which had been transformed from the seat of royalty to a public museum after the Revolution, was arranged. The expedition would include, of course, Célestine, who was as enchanted as her brother with the cheerful girl who appeared to be so much at ease in their company.

As for the three older people, they were delighted with their evening's work, Monsieur and Madame Cabarroques because they felt that the handsome young lieutenant might be sufficiently attracted to their daughter to make him want to bestow upon her his name and title, and the Countess because she foresaw the possibility of restoring the d'Albert family fortunes. Who can blame them for their ambitious plans? Life can indeed be tasteless without an aspiration or two.

Alain's leave was to last for four weeks. At the end of two he had decided that marriage to Marie-Josèphe offered every possibility of bliss, and after a fortnight of her delightful and almost constant companionship, it only remained for him to make his proposal. Confident that his addresses would be welcome to all concerned, that is to say to the young lady herself and to her parents, he chose to make an afternoon call upon the Cabarroques at their house in the Rue Geoffroy St. Hilaire and requested permission of Monsieur Cabarroques to take his daughter for a walk in the *Jardin des*

Plantes, which was situated close by. Permission was readily granted and was accompanied by the most indulgent of smiles from Madame Cabarroques, whose face reflected every shade of emotion displayed on the boisterous features of her husband.

As the two young people emerged from the house and descended a short flight of steps into the street, Alain offered Marie-Josèphe his arm; it was immediately accepted without a trace of embarrassment. He felt foolishly protective towards her. The small gloved hand, resting so trustingly in the crook of his elbow, gave him a sense of responsibility; it was as though he alone stood between Marie-Josèphe and the unpredictable hazards of an uncertain world. He had never felt this way about Christina.

The memory of his mistress occasioned a slight feeling of unease. He brushed it aside. It would need but a moment of time in which to tell her that she was no longer to be a part of his life, an awkward moment to be sure, but one he had long anticipated.

The *Jardin des Plantes* was full of Sunday walkers, well-wrapped against the chill wind of early spring. Fashion was not yet much in evidence, depending as it did on more clement weather. Elegance was forsaken in favour of warmth.

Weaving in and out of their elders, children in fur hats bowled forbidden iron-rimmed hoops over the frost-hardened paths, risking chastisement as they 'shaved' the legs of some luckless pedestrian. It was a pleasant, animated scene, far removed from the horrors of a distant battlefield and a thousand personal tragedies. Alain had been a soldier for nine years and had spent little time, apart from a few months following the receipt of his commission, in the company of intelligent, cultivated women, a fact which had never bothered him until now. It had been easy enough to take the decision to ask Marie-Josèphe to marry him, but sooner or later decisions have to be implemented and to implement this one required more nerve than facing a battery of sixteen-pounders. He had never felt so devoid of initiative.

While her escort was hard at work summoning up his reserves of courage, Marie-Josèphe, who had the capacity to enjoy the abundance of simple pleasures which life has to offer, was admiring some Pasque flowers which had just come into bloom in the borders lining the path. Blatant as courtesans in full array, they nodded their crimson and purple heads at the passers-by.

Marie-Josèphe seemed entirely unconscious of Alain's dilemma as she drew his attention to the shrubs and plants and gave them their Latin names. 'These are called *Pulsatilla Vulgaris*,' she said, pointing to the Pasque flowers. 'Are they not beautiful?'

'I am not familiar with the names of botanical specimens,' he replied awkwardly. 'I never had time to study the subject.'

'But you are able to observe, and are not afraid to venture an opinion as to whether you find them pleasing to the eye?'

'Well then, yes, they are very pleasing.'

Her lips parted in a smile. 'Good. I am glad that we are in accord upon such an important matter.'

'May we reach agreement on something else?'

'Perhaps we may. What shall it be?'

'Shall we accept the fact that when two people are in love the sensible thing for them to do is to get married?'

She had her head turned away from him now and he could not see her face under the lilac silk bonnet, but he felt her hand tighten on his arm and was encouraged to proceed. 'I am not much good at speech-making, Mademoiselle Cabarroques. Soldiers in general are a taciturn breed, but if the words 'I love you' are sufficient to convince you that my heart is yours, will you do me the honour of becoming my wife?'

She drew to a halt and turned to face him. The blue eyes were radiant with joy and his heart gave a great leap. 'Your words, Lieutenant, are convincing enough and the sentiments contained therein are most heartily reciprocated. I think we shall be extraordinarily happy together.'

He was so relieved that he began to laugh and she joined in, without quite knowing what she was laughing at. They walked on, drawing closer together, maintaining a sweet silence as each savoured this moment of supreme happiness.

A small arbour, enclosing a wooden bench, caught Alain's eye. He steered Marie-Joséphe towards it and they sat down, their bodies touching. He took her hand.

'Forgive me,' he said, 'but is it not customary for young ladies to refuse a proposal of marriage the first time it is made, just to make the lover more frantic?'

She arched her brows at him. 'Would you have preferred me to do that?'

He shook his head. 'Not at all. I was merely curious to know if what I had heard was true.'

'In some cases I have no doubt that it is so, but to follow convention slavishly when one is in love is surely a sign of a weak mind, if not of a mischievous disposition.'

'I agree. Convention, while contributing to an ordered society, can produce an inflexibility which is not at all desirable, especially when it reduces frantic lovers to gibbering wrecks.'

She squeezed his hand. 'Now that we are of the same mind for the second time today, I give you permission to play the lover and tell me when you first decided that I should make a tolerably useful soldier's wife.'

He bent upon her a look of astonishment. 'A soldier's wife? My expectation was that you would ask me to resign my commission and become a country gentleman.'

'Why should I expect you to give up a career which you have chosen to pursue and which satisfies the dictates of your nature?'

'Because I thought the fair sex were repelled by the very notion of war.'

(*War is cruel . . .* ' *Christina at her most stubborn*).

'The only thing that repels me is the idea of a man sacrificing his career on the whim of a selfish woman.'

He leant towards her and planted a chaste kiss on her cheek. 'I have never met any woman quite like you, my dear. You continually surprise me.'

'Have you known many women?'

(The word 'known' carried infinite possibilities of interpretation).

He replied candidly, 'A few. You would not expect it to be otherwise?'

'No. I have not reached the age of three and twenty without having some knowledge of the world.'

To his relief she abandoned the subject of his past. 'Would it surprise you to learn that my parents have been waiting with bated breath for you to propose to me? I fear they have been seduced by the delightful prospect of my becoming a countess.'

He pretended to look hurt. 'And I was under the impression that they liked me for the laudable qualities which they have discovered I possess. For example, I never wear dirty boots.'

She laughed up at him. 'Of course they like you. They are the dearest people in the world. As for the title, if it would not distress you, I think I should prefer to be plain Madame d'Albert.'

'Distress me? Quite the contrary, I assure you. My rank in the army of France is satisfaction enough for me. My mother, I know, refers to me as 'my son, the Count,' but I cannot reproach her for that. All that I am today I owe to the strength and courage she showed during the darkest period of her life. It pleases her to be reminded of the old, leisured days when our family and others like us did not have to pay our rent on this earth.'

A moment of silence preceded his own confession. 'Would it surprise *you* if I told you that my mother is anxious for me to marry a well-dowered lady, and that she too has been hoping that we shall make a match of it?'

She lowered her head as the colour crept into her cheeks. 'Dear me. I perceive it is a time for honesty between us.'

The moment of embarrassment passed and her well-developed sense of humour came to the fore. 'I had hoped that the Countess liked me for the laudable qualities which she has discovered I possess.'

He managed a smile, but his face wore an expression of concern. 'I hope you do not believe that my proposal to you was influenced in any way by financial considerations? And before you answer, let me add that until quite recently I did propose to choose a rich wife, without deeming it necessary to fall in love, but that was before I met you and I now realise that it was both arrogant and unfeeling of me to think that such a thing would be possible in my case. If I did not love you I could not, in all conscience, marry you, not even if your father was as rich as Croesus. As to my mother's feelings towards you, it is not too much to say that she is in the process of developing a strong affection for one whom she holds in the highest possible esteem.'

If his words sounded patronizing she was willing to overlook this fact in the springtime of her love, but a mild rebuke could not be resisted. 'There is no need to be so earnest in your protestations. If you had been lying when you told me that you loved me I should have known it.'

He thought this amusing. 'By what means?'

'People flutter their eyelids when they are about to tell a falsehood. It is a sure sign of deceit.'

'You are probably right. The exception, they say, proves the rule.

The most accomplished liar in my regiment is my sergeant and he looks me straight in the eye when he is about to stretch my credulity to the limit without so much as a single flicker of his eyelashes.'

They collapsed into laughter and as lovers will, spoke of inconsequential things before returning to the Rue Geoffroy St. Hilaire to inform a delighted Monsieur and Madame Cabarroques that it was their wish to become husband and wife.

The Countess was equally delighted when she heard the news. 'Now,' she declared, addressing her smiling son, 'you will be able to live in some style with that beautiful, good-natured girl.'

'And I shall have a dear sister,' put in Célestine, earning a fond kiss from her brother.

6

Strasbourg
April, 1806

When his month's leave was up Alain went back to Strasbourg to take out a lease on a suitable house for himself and his bride to move into after the celebration of their marriage, which was due to take place in Paris in May. He did not anticipate that his colonel would withhold permission for him to marry, but he had warned Marie-Josèphe that a wedding-tour would be considered inappropriate in wartime, 'in case affairs come to the boil while we are away,' as he graphically expressed it. As it happened, Alain was not called upon to fight again until the following September, the Emperor having spent the best part of the year 1806 raising his brothers, Joseph and Louis Bonaparte, to the dignity of kings — and, as he admitted himself, turning them into enemies he had to watch out for — and appointing himself as Protector of the Confederation of German States.

Alain was not looking forward to his meeting with Christina which, being a man of honour, he could scarcely avoid. In any case he had no desire to leave loose ends untied. That she would be shocked by his sudden decision to marry he could not doubt. She might even believe that his trip to Paris had been designed for that very purpose, and that he had deliberately concealed his intention from her. Had not their last conversation together been concerned with the subject of marriage? His fervent hope was that she would accept the inevitable and not start a quarrel. It was a hope ill-founded on his previous experience of her.

A few seconds after he entered the house in the square which had been his home for two years, he was in the process of breathing a sigh of relief that the portly figure of Madame La Harpe was nowhere in evidence, when the lady herself popped into view from behind her sitting-room door like an Austrian sniper emerging from the cover of a hedge. She gave him as much of a fright.

'Madame La Harpe!' he exclaimed, trying to inject a note of gratification into his voice. 'How are you?'

She waddled forward with her pink cheeks wobbling and her little black eyes glistening with pleasure. 'Oh, Monsieur, I am very well, I thank the good God, and if you will forgive the liberty, your appearance has changed greatly for the better since I saw you last. Your holiday has done you good.'

'Thank you, Madame, I feel very much better,' he confirmed and set his foot upon the stair.

Madame's glance travelled upwards. 'She is waiting for you, your lady, and so pretty and neat. She will make someone a good wife, that one.'

Alain could not resist the urge to challenge this statement. 'I thought you said she had the Devil in her eyes?'

Madame chuckled obscenely. 'I think you have chased him away, Monsieur.'

He climbed the stairs slowly, consciously delaying the moment of his meeting with Christina, and aware that moral cowardice is as much to be despised as that other form of cowardice which he had witnessed more than once on the field of battle. As he reached the first landing he looked down and saw Madame La Harpe's face upturned towards him like a round pink moon. The hot, speculative eyes disgusted him. He plodded on, his boots making a loud clatter on the wooden treads, until he reached the third landing and the familiar, brown-painted door. He took a deep breath before placing his hand on the brass knob which turned with a protesting squeak.

She was sitting sewing, with her work-basket on the table before her and a length of white linen in her hands. Behind her on the small stove, an iron cooking-pot bubbled away and sent forth a tempting aroma which made his nostrils twitch. She turned her head as he entered and he saw the artificial flower of yellow velvet tucked discreetly into the dark, piled-up hair, a complement to the neat, high-waisted dress of fawn silk with its puffed sleeves and white lace collar.

Her greeting was more restrained than usual and there was nothing hurried about her movements as she put aside her work, rose from her chair and came towards him. She might have been a wife welcoming her husband home, except that she did not offer her cheek to be kissed, but just stood looking at him with her large, questioning eyes. He had the absurd feeling that she was waiting for him to explain to her his every movement since he had left her a month ago.

A banal remark rose to his lips. 'Something smells good.'

'I am cooking to a recipe only

recently invented,' she replied gravely. 'The Emperor's cook devised it after the battle of Marengo when the food stocks were low. He had some onions and almonds in his stores and he picked a few mushrooms to concoct a meal which has now become the Emperor's favourite dish. It is called Chicken Marengo. I made it today because the soldiers have been streaming into Strasbourg since early morning and I thought you would come.'

His face wore the uncertain smile of a man harbouring a dark secret. 'You are well informed about the Emperor's culinary habits.'

Her smile was as muted as her manner. 'The recipe was printed in '*Le Temps*,' with details of how it was invented.' She motioned towards the bedroom. 'There is hot water on the stove and I have put out soap and a clean towel. Go and have a wash. By the time you have finished the meal will be ready.'

He should have told her there and

then. Instead, he was allowing her to envelop him once more in her cocoon of cosy domesticity.

By the time he came back into the outer room she had set the table and was serving the meal with her usual deftness and economy of movement. Almost before he had time to address the generous portion of chicken which reposed on his plate she began asking him about his mother and sister, prompting him to expand on the social activities he had pursued while he was in Paris.

'Did you go to the opera? It said in one of the newspapers that Glück's 'Alceste' was being performed in Paris, with Talma singing the leading rôle.'

'Yes, we did go to the opera,' he confirmed and wondered why the food seemed so tasteless.

'Does the Countess prefer the opera to the theatre?'

'No, I think the theatre is her first love. *Maman* prefers her music without the intrusion of the human voice.'

'If she is not fond of singing, why does she go to the opera?'

'To conform to the popular taste.'

She thought about this for a moment before replying, 'If singing was detestable to me I should not go to the opera just to conform.'

'Really? You surprise me. I thought conformity was the shrine at which you worshipped. If you are to become respectable you must learn to do things which are not always to your taste.'

'How can I do things not to my taste when I never get a chance to find out what my taste is? I think my preference would lie with the theatre, but since I may not go to a play I am not in a position to state an opinion.'

'Who says you may not go to a play?'

'*You* will not escort me to the theatre.'

'You know why that is, but there is nothing to stop you going with Emil and Elise.'

Her jaw dropped and she pushed

aside her plate. 'If Emil is not ashamed to be seen with me, why then are you?'

He sighed impatiently. 'I repeat, you *know* why. We have been through all this a hundred times. Really, Christina, coming home to you is like resuming a conversation which has just been broken off. Do I have to remind you again that there are certain people in the regiment who know my family, whereas in the case of Emil . . . '

She interrupted him furiously. 'Whereas Emil is only the son of a tailor. You, however, are the son of an aristocrat, and I thought all that rubbish about levels of society went out with the Revolution. Men lost their heads for holding views like yours, Alain.'

'I know.'

The sadness conveyed in those two words was lost on her and she rounded off her rebuke with, 'I suppose now that Bonaparte has made himself an emperor, France is falling back into her old bad habits.'

Given a change of emphasis it was more or less what his mother had said. He had no inclination to continue the argument. His lips felt stiff, as if they too had begun to rebel against these senseless, laboured exchanges. He could not put off his confession a moment longer.

'Christina, I have something to tell you.'

She had pulled back her plate and was eating again. Despite his mental confusion and lack of appetite he had to admit that the Chicken Marengo was really very good. The tastelessness had been occasioned by his own lack of backbone.

'Something pleasant?'

'I fear you will not find it so.'

She looked up from her plate and he could see that he had frightened her. He forced himself to go on. There was no easy way to break bad news. 'While I was on leave in Paris I was introduced to a lady who is to become my wife.'

He had expected her to erupt with anger as soon as the words were out of his mouth, but she simply lowered her head and digested the information in silence, pushing the food around on her plate and stabbing at it now and then with her fork. A minute or two passed before she asked without looking at him, 'Is she old and ugly?'

'No, she is young and very beautiful.'

Her cheeks went a deep, fiery red. 'And rich?'

'And possessed of a considerable fortune, yes.'

'Then it must be your title she covets.'

'It does not occur to you that the lady may be in love with me, and I with her?'

'I think it is not usual for two people to fall in love so quickly. There must be an interest on both sides. Her desire is to become a countess and yours to become a rich count.'

'Well,' said he, 'I shall not endeavour to convince you that such is not the case, since it is plain to me that you have no wish to believe in the goodness of human nature.'

At this, she flung down her napkin, scraped back her chair and hurried over to the window, where she sat down and almost at once began to cry. It was really no worse than he had expected. He gritted his teeth and steeled himself to endure the scene which he knew must be the price of his desertion of her.

The first onslaught was not long delayed. 'You went to Paris to look for an heiress. All that stuff about wanting to see your mother and sister was a lie, to keep me from suspecting your true purpose.' She began mopping at her eyes with her handkerchief. 'Are you too much of a coward to admit it?'

He poured himself a glass of wine. 'I shall admit to nothing which is not true. The lady in question and her parents have been friends of my mother and sister for some time. They were invited to dinner during my stay, but

111

before I went to Paris I had no thought of finding a wife, as you put it, and was not even aware of the existence of the family to whom I was introduced.'

He wondered why he was bothering to defend himself. In his estimation he owed her nothing, not even an explanation of his rapid courtship of Marie-Josèphe.

'Have you told her about me?'

'I believe I have already made my thoughts plain on that subject.'

'Yes, you said it would be a foolish thing to do.'

'If not downright stupid.'

She threatened childishly, 'What if I decide to tell her myself?'

'I should not advise it. You may think that you have it in your power to do me harm, but you would be well advised to remember that it is within my power to return the compliment.'

'What does that mean?'

'It means that if envy should get the better of you and you make it your business to meddle in my affairs, I shall not hesitate to return injury for injury. I have only to bring a complaint before the *Chef de Police* of Strasbourg and he will have you drummed out of this city without giving you time to gather up your possessions. The status of a soldier's woman is little above that of a vagrant.'

'Your word as an officer and a gentleman against my word as a whore,' she said bitterly. 'What would you tell the *Chef de Police*, that I had stolen your money?'

'Perhaps I should tell him the truth, that you tried to blackmail me.'

Her lip quivered. 'I beg you not to leave me, Alain.'

'You know I must.'

'We could still see each other.'

'No, we could not.' He spoke firmly. 'We have been over this ground before. Many men have mistresses, you will say. Yes, that is true, but I am not the sort of man who needs more than one woman in his life. I have been faithful to *you* for almost a year.'

'If I had been rich and from a good family, would you have married me?'

'That is hard to say,' he answered coldly. 'Sometimes I think you are far too opinionated to make any man a good wife and that there is nothing in this world which could escape the lash of your tongue. As a soldier's woman you do well enough. You at least have the ability to make a man laugh.'

These words were a dreadful blow to her pride, but Christina could never resist the temptation to prolong an argument.

'I should have thought that was an excellent quality in a wife.'

'There you are quite wrong. One cannot survive on laughter alone. There must be other, more enduring, qualities to attach two people together.'

'Which I do not possess?'

'Which you do not possess. You skim the cream off the surface of life, Christina, ignoring everything which either does not please you or does not suit your notions of what constitutes

114

a perfect world. When I present you with an irrefutable fact which you would rather not face up to, you immediately turn the conversation and go careering off in pursuit of some other crack-brained idea which is more to your taste. Applying such a character as yours to the state of matrimony, I think you would make a very indifferent mother. Every time your baby cried you would stuff your fingers into your ears and run away, instead of shouldering your maternal responsibilities and giving care and comfort to a creature in distress. My advice to you is to find another protector and go on doing the thing you are best at.'

A long, long silence fell between them. She, he was relieved to discover, did not seem predisposed to work herself up into a fit of hysterics over his cold and pompous appraisal of her character. One must be thankful for small mercies. It was time to get down to practicalities. He said, 'I will give you some money before I go, a sum to tide you over and give you time to make other arrangements.'

'Time to find another soldier to take me on?'

'It would seem the most sensible thing for you to do, only next time choose an elderly colonel. You will get more out of him.'

She sat with her head bowed in an attitude of utter despair. Her hands were perfectly still now. She might have been carved out of stone. Alain's calculatedly cruel words hammered at his conscience and he became aware of a sharp pang of self-disgust. He dared not make any move to comfort her, however, lest she envelop him again in her smothering possessiveness. In time she would forget him.

He rose from the table. 'I must go.'

Her head came up and she turned to face him, with her blue eyes wide open and alarmed. 'You can stay here tonight.'

'I do not think that would be a good idea.'

She said softly, 'I am just a soldier's woman, Alain. You may still need me now and again, even after you have entered the holy state of matrimony. Wives are not always as accommodating as mistresses. They sometimes get moody, especially when they are pregnant. Strasbourg is full of whores, of course, but it would be safer for you to come to me. My body is clean.'

Her eyes pleaded with him. 'Please stay, Alain. I promise not to say another word to make you uneasy.'

His smile was rueful. 'I strongly doubt that.'

He made love to her that night with the shadow of Marie-Josèphe hovering over him. With her sharp, feminine instinct Christina sensed that he had already distanced himself from her, and when the final, meaningless coming together was over, she turned her back on him and fell asleep on the lumpy mattress with the suddenness of a child.

The next morning Alain woke at dawn and put on his clothes with the minimum of disturbance. He stole out of the house in the square like a thief, leaving behind him nothing but a faint animal smell and one hundred francs.

7

Strasbourg
Summer, 1806

Married life agreed with Alain. He put on weight and had to take his uniform to the regimental tailor to have the seams let out. The access to almost unlimited funds — Monsieur Cabarroques had generously dowered his daughter with one hundred and twenty thousand francs per annum — opened up new horizons for him. He and Marie-Josèphe now lived in a large, comfortably furnished house, well away from the old part of the town, and in the jargon of the day — applied only to the well-off — 'kept their own carriage.'

In addition to the carriage-horses the d'Albert stables housed two well-bred hunters and a docile gelding for Marie-Josèphe, who did not excel at equestrian pursuits.

The newly-married pair gave dinner-parties every week, to which they invited their friends, mostly officers of the 7th Hussars, who came with their wives or visiting female relatives.

Emil became a frequent caller at the house in the Rue du Loup, where his hostess plied him with the fine French food prepared by her chef and offered him a choice of the best château-bottled wines. Marie-Josèphe adopted a determinedly maternal attitude towards the cheerful hussar which he found quite charming. He thought his friend Alain the luckiest fellow alive.

One of the most gratifying moments of Alain's new life came when his mother and sister arrived from Paris to take up permanent residence in his house. He had become a family man at last and his cup was full. It ran over when his wife announced that she was to have a child.

There was no renewal of hostilities between France and her enemies during that summer of 1806 and Alain had much free time on his hands, his duties as a lieutenant consisting mainly of turning up at morning and afternoon parades and putting young cavalrymen through their paces. An occasional review in the fields outside the town varied the monotony. In his off-duty periods he and Marie-Josèphe visited friends, or went for outings into the country in their smart new carriage. The evenings were taken up with excursions to the opera and to the theatre.

Sometimes, when Marie-Josèphe was visiting her female acquaintances, Alain would go riding with Emil, or perhaps the two would visit one of their old haunts for a drink and conversation. By tacit consent the Café Violette was avoided. On a few occasions Elise would be present at these convivial têtes-à-têtes and would shyly enquire after the health of Marie-Josèphe, a courtesy to which Alain would respond with equal politeness, adding that his wife had asked to be remembered to her.

Unspoken between them was the unpalatable fact that in this post-revolutionary world, class distinction had once more reared its head, making it impossible for a married woman to invite a soldier's woman to her house. Marie-Josèphe, to whom such distinctions were anathema, had actually suggested to her husband that an invitation to Emil to dinner should be extended to his girl-friend, but the proposal had been firmly vetoed with a remark to the effect that one must draw the line somewhere. At this, Marie-Josèphe had accused Alain of being stuffy and had spent the rest of the day addressing him as '*Monsieur le Comte*,' but with her usual tact, she had not insisted on having her own way. However, she had concluded their discussion by saying, 'Perhaps one day Emil will marry Elise and then we can all be friends.' The idea had been dismissed as improbable, producing the teasing but nonetheless telling rejoinder, 'Why should he not? You married beneath you, my dearest.'

Marie-Josèphe's verbal messages always made Elise blush fiercely. Alain never understood why. He was unable to grasp the concept of a deep humiliation caused by the fact that the wife of one with whom the good-natured girl had been on familiar terms for several years, could not allow herself to be seen in the company of a soldier's woman.

It was Emil who first spotted Christina hanging about outside the Café Edelweiss in the Rue de Venise. Alain's former mistress had stationed herself in the doorway of a boutique directly opposite the café and had stepped back hurriedly into the shadows as the two hussars emerged one afternoon in early August. She was not quite quick enough to avoid detection.

Emil made no mention of his discovery until he and Alain had proceeded some way up the street. A quick glance over his shoulder revealed only a busy thoroughfare thronged with unfamiliar faces.

'Did you see her?'

'Who?' Alain had stopped to inspect some boots in a shop window.

'Christina. She was standing in the doorway of the hat boutique, opposite the café.'

Alain shrugged and moved on. 'So? She was probably choosing a hat.'

'No, she was standing quite still, looking towards the café. I think she had been there for some time. She disappeared fast enough when she caught sight of us.'

Alain frowned. 'Why should she be interested in who comes and goes in the café?'

'How the hell do I know?'

'Well, whatever she was doing does not concern us. Our appearance probably took her by surprise and she felt too embarrassed to acknowledge our presence. She and I did not part on the happiest of terms.'

'I expect that was it,' replied Emil and promptly dismissed the matter from his mind.

As the summer wore on and Marie-Josèphe's pregnancy began to exact its toll of her energy, Alain saw rather more of Emil and rather less of his wife, who had been instructed by her physician to rest and who remained at home in the afternoons, whiling away the long hours with novels and endless games of solitaire.

Having completed his regimental duties by midday, Alain would return home for a meal and after seeing Marie-Josèphe comfortably disposed on her chaise-longue, with her instruments of diversion at hand, would fill in the time before afternoon parade at garrison headquarters in the company of his fellow-officers and a pack of cards.

About a week after Emil's sighting of Christina she turned up again. This time Alain saw her himself, walking along in front of him in the Rue de Venise and stopping now and then to window-gaze. Not wanting to pass her and risk a confrontation, he slowed down and lingered before a shop window until she had turned the corner ahead.

From that time on Christina's appearances, always at some little distance, but well within view, became more and more frequent until not a day passed when Alain did not catch sight of her tall, slender figure with its studiedly averted face. Even when he went riding along beside the river towards the village of Sélestat, accompanied by other eager equestrians, she was there, mounted on an indifferent horse which she had obviously hired. The thought that she must have somehow acquired a prior knowledge of his movements alarmed him.

'She is spying on you, old fellow,' declared Emil, who had been a fascinated witness to most of Christina's manifestations. 'You may depend upon it.'

The two friends were enjoying a game of euchre in the officers' mess.

Alain examined his hand of cards with an appearance of great concentration, but his thoughts were elsewhere. 'I wonder if that is what she meant when she said she would never let me go? After I told her that I was to be married and that our relationship was at an end, she said a number of foolish things, among which was a remark about haunting me.'

He slapped his forehead. 'No, no, that was not it . . . *hunting* was the word she used. She said she would hunt me down.'

Emil gave a brief, puzzled laugh. 'I always thought Christina had butterflies in her head where her common sense should be. Take my advice and put a stop to this nonsense before it gets out of control.'

'What do you mean, before it gets out of control?' Alain lowered the hand holding his cards like a man lowering his guard. He was beginning to look worried.

Emil reached across the table to give

him a fatherly pat on the shoulder. 'Look at the facts, old fellow. Christina, probably as part of some deep-laid scheme of her own devising, is following you about. First of all she turns up occasionally, then she steps up her operation until she is turning up every day. What do you suppose her next move will be?'

Alain slapped down the King of Hearts. 'God alone knows. Perhaps she will prostrate herself at my feet in full view of the public at large. I would not put anything past her.'

'All the more reason for you to take the bull by the horns and nip in the bud any form of outlandish display. Find out what it is she wants. There is bound to be something . . . money perhaps?' Emil added a warning. 'But do not, I beg you, approach her in the streets. She may make a scene. Go back to your old lodgings and talk to Madame La Harpe. My bet is that Christina is still occupying your rooms.'

Alain took his friend's advice the very next day. As he walked across the familiar square with the sun beating down on his face, a sudden sensation of sadness swept over him and he wondered why this should be so. But even as he told himself that he did not regret the passing of his former life, a feeling of nostalgia for the old irresponsible and disordered days took possession of him. The mind is fond of playing such tricks.

By the time he reached the door of No. 42, Rue du Dôme, the feeling had gone. With her usual precognition Madame La Harpe emerged from her sitting-room at the exact moment Alain pushed his way through the half-opened door and set foot in the hallway of the house. She seemed less than delighted to see him. Following form, she lowered her spectacles, but her round, fat face showed no sign of creasing into a smile.

Alain was puzzled by this frosty reception, but he was in no mood to pursue the whys and wherefores of Madame's strangely altered attitude towards him. His business was with Christina. Formality was met with formality.

'Is Mademoiselle Calvi still living here, Madame?'

Her chin gave a little jerk which he interpreted as a sign of assent.

'Is she at home?'

The marionette-like action was repeated.

'May I go up?'

The request was followed by a long, considering silence, broken by the chilly statement, 'I will see if Mademoiselle Calvi wishes to receive you, Monsieur.'

Madame brushed by the fallen hero and with absurd dignity began the long, slow climb to the third floor, ascending heavenwards like the goddess of fury. Alain watched the swishing black skirt and gleaming half-boots with a jaundiced eye and contained his anger. An altercation with Madame

La Harpe would have been the last straw.

Five minutes passed before he heard the thump of feet descending the stairs. A moment or so later he was informed, with impressive dignity, that Mademoiselle Calvi was at home and would receive him.

'Stupid old witch,' muttered Alain under his breath and taking the stairs two at a time, knocked on Christina's door. She opened it at once, smiled a greeting and stood back invitingly.

'Alain! How glad I am to see you.'

'This is not a social call,' he snapped and strode into the room which seemed to him to have shrunk since he last saw it. Its shabbiness appalled him.

'How well you look,' she remarked, still with that same bright, welcoming smile. 'I can see that marriage agrees with you.'

The pleasantry was ignored. He stood in the centre of the room, looking large and threatening in his uniform. 'Why are you following me?'

She made no attempt to deny the charge but replied calmly, 'Because it helps me to become reconciled to your rejection of me. I have discovered that if I can see you now and then it eases for me the pain of our parting. I cannot explain why this should be because I have always been led to believe that it is better not to open old wounds. I beg you not to be angry with me.'

The plea had no softening effect. 'Now and then, you say? For God's sake, I cannot step out of doors without falling over you.'

'I did not mean to upset you.'

'You have not upset me. Being upset is a thing to which only females are addicted, but you have certainly angered me. And what have you been saying to Madame La Harpe? She looked as though it would have given her the greatest possible pleasure to plunge a knife into my heart.'

'Madame thinks you have treated me badly.'

If a man can be said to swell with

indignation Alain did so now, drawing himself up to his full height and pushing out his chest. 'Oh, so Madame thinks that, does she? Well, let me tell you that she never thought that about the other three girls I had before you came along to bedevil my existence. What is so different about you?'

'Madame says I am not like the others. She says she thought you would marry me.'

Alain's eyes blazed. 'The presumptuous old baggage. And I suppose you did nothing to disabuse her of such an absurd idea. Indeed, I believe you to be quite capable of giving it birth.'

She denied this, but her colour rose as she went on to repeat yet more of Madame's philosophy. 'Madame says you have behaved towards me like a pre-revolutionary aristocrat, and that you should realise that times have changed. Everyone is equal in France today.'

'If you believe that you are a bigger fool than I imagined,' he returned savagely. 'Our head of state is an emperor now, not a jumped-up official of the Committee of Public Safety who sends people to the guillotine for the crime of being born into the *noblesse.*'

'It was the Emperor himself who drew up the Civil Code which provides for equality for all under the law and an end to feudal rights and duties,' she pointed out. 'Can you deny that?'

'Still the same old Christina,' he sneered, 'quoting chapter and verse at me. You should have joined the army. It is full of barrack-room lawyers.'

He looked about him at the miserable room. It was as neat and clean as she could make it. 'Do you mean to stay here?'

'For the time being. I have taken up a position as governess to the children of Captain Bessières. I go daily to teach them to speak Italian.'

Captain Bessières, a man who had begun life as a surgeon's assistant, was well-known to Alain. He said uneasily,

'I hope you have made no mention of your connection with me?'

Her reply infuriated him. 'He knew of it already and was not inclined to blame me for living with a man whom I had fully expected to marry, or to consider that I was not a fit person to instruct his children. I have received nothing but kindness at the hands of Captain Bessières and his wife.'

'I can believe that. Perhaps they too think I should be strung up on the nearest *lanterne*.' He made a conscious effort to control his anger. 'I am straying from the purpose of my visit, which is to request that you will refrain from making your presence felt on every occasion when it pleases me to appear in public.'

'And if I refuse to comply with your request, will you make good your threat and report me to the *Chef de Police*?'

'If you persist in harassing me I shall have no alternative but to do so.'

'I have as much right to be seen on

the streets of this city as have you.'

He lifted his shoulders in contemptuous dismissal of this claim. 'I see that you are determined to have your own way, so I will save my breath, but if it is war you want, then war you shall have. I will not be bested by a woman.'

With that he was gone, slamming the door behind him before clattering down the stairs. Madame La Harpe stood foursquare in the hallway and glared at him as he skirted his way round her.

★ ★ ★

In the days and weeks which followed his confrontation with Christina the situation worsened for Alain. It began to be rumoured in the regiment that he had jilted a respectable woman in order to marry a woman of substance, and one or two officers who had accepted his hospitality no longer did so. The rest cared little one way or the other, and the wild stories being circulated about him did Alain only the minimum of harm.

They did come to the ears of his colonel, however, along with the intriguing information that Lieutenant d'Albert's former mistress was hanging about in the vicinity of his house and generally making a nuisance of herself.

Colonel Varesne, a man of rigid moral principles, did not like the idea that one of his officers was getting a reputation for being a rake and summoned the culprit to his office to explain himself. A stiff, upright little man with narrow features and white hair which stood up like a brush on his head, Varesne had first seen service at the battle of Valmy in 1792, serving in the army of Louis XVI. He was what might be called a middle-of-the-road revolutionary.

Varesne was nothing if not direct. Alain's salute was barely completed before a demand was trumpeted forth: 'What the devil is going on between you and this Calvi female, d'Albert?'

His subordinate stood to attention on the uncarpeted floor and pleaded his innocence. 'Nothing, sir. Nothing is going on between myself and Mademoiselle Calvi. She was my mistress before I married Madame d'Albert.'

The information was superfluous. 'She comes from a family of some substance, I am given to understand. It is reported that her father was a magistrate in Turin.'

'That is Mademoiselle Calvi's claim, yes.'

'Do I detect a note of incredulity in your tone, d'Albert? Have you any reason to suppose that the lady is not telling the truth about her father?'

'Every reason, sir. She is very much inclined towards exaggeration. When I first met Mademoiselle Calvi she told me that she had become a soldier's woman from choice. Now, however, she denies this and holds herself up to public view as the injured party in our affair, insisting that I offered her marriage which, on my word of honour as a gentleman, I did not. To add insult to injury, Mademoiselle Calvi has begun to follow me about.'

Alain forced a brittle laugh. 'To tell the truth, sir, I am beginning to fear her presence more than a whole company of charging Austrian dragoons.'

Varesne's frown indicated that this was not a matter for levity. 'Following you about?' he repeated. 'I never heard of such a thing. Are you quite certain that you are not allowing your imagination to run away with you, d'Albert?'

'No, sir!' Alain permitted himself a spurt of righteous indignation before adding stiffly, 'If the colonel requires confirmation of my statement he has only to apply to Lieutenant Emil Durand, who has been a witness to many of Mademoiselle Calvi's embarrassing appearances.'

Varesne's expression was bemused.

'It is certainly not the action of a lady,' he conceded.

Encouraged by this sign that credibility might be considered to be on his side, Alain added, 'She even follows me when I go riding.'

The dawn of amusement rose in the steady grey eyes of the older man. 'How does she manage that? I suppose you do not write to her, informing her of the exact time of your proposed mounted excursions?'

The young man appeared to take the question seriously. 'No, sir. I have no idea how she manages it.'

'She may be in league with one of your servants, or she may have tricked one of them into revealing details of your movements,' the colonel suggested helpfully.

'I had thought of that, sir. I am looking into the possibility.'

Varesne gazed long and hard at a miniature of his wife which reposed in its gold oval frame on his desk and thanked God for the wisdom of five and forty years, when a man's blood ran cooler and in more placid streams. His glance transferred itself to Alain as he pronounced judgment.

'I thought at first that your behaviour had been less than gentlemanly, d'Albert, but I am prepared to accept your explanation that Mademoiselle Calvi is nothing but a common soldier's woman.' He chuckled drily. 'Or perhaps I should say uncommon. She is something quite beyond my experience. However, it does not look good for the regiment to have one of its officers made a fool of by a woman.'

'But what am I to do, sir?' Alain tried hard to subdue the note of desperation in his voice. 'Mademoiselle Calvi is acting as governess to the children of Captain Bessières. What worries me more than anything is the fact that some unpleasant stories may reach the ears of my wife.'

'Madame d'Albert knows nothing of your relationship with Mademoiselle Calvi?'

'Nothing.'

'Then I advise you to tell her about it before someone else gives her a distorted view of the matter. As to having Mademoiselle Calvi forcibly ejected from Strasbourg, I agree with you that such a course would be neither practicable nor wise. For the moment, I think it best to rest on the hope that the lady will grow tired of her own unacceptable behaviour.'

Alain took his commanding officer's advice and told Marie-Josèphe of his former relationship with Christina. Her reaction to his tale both relieved and surprised him. Reclining on her chaise-longue, book in hand, and looking, he thought, more beautiful than ever in a white silk morning dress frilled with blue satin, and with her hair dressed in the Grecian style with blue ribbon bands, Marie-Josèphe regarded his anxious countenance with tolerant blue eyes.

'Poor woman. You should feel sorry for her, Alain.'

Could he credit the evidence of his own ears? 'Sorry?'

'Yes, it is obvious to me that she loves you very much.'

'You do not understand. She wants to get inside my head.'

'What a strange thing to say.'

He sighed. 'You do not know her.'

She waited for him to elaborate on his cryptic observation, but all he said was, 'Marie-Josèphe, you must believe me when I say that Christina Calvi meant nothing to me. She is just a soldier's woman.'

'Why did you not tell me about her before?'

'I thought you might not understand my reasons for setting up home with a woman I did not wish to marry.'

'How very narrow-minded of you, my dearest.'

'Yes, it was. I might have guessed that you would take the rounded view.'

She laughed. 'By that I suppose you mean that I am morally suspect?'

'Not at all. I meant only that you are

the sort of person who sees all sides of a question and does not presume to stand in judgment upon your fellow human-beings. I wish I had your depth of perception.'

'Thank you. I take that as a very pretty compliment.' She tilted her head. 'At least, I think I do. There is one school of thought which attributes depth of perception to old men who linger too long over the port after dinner.'

This elicited a faint smile. 'If only I could think of some way of removing her permanently from my life.'

'You could leave her to me.'

'To you?'

'Yes, I could go to see her. Faced with the flesh and blood reality of her defeat, she may be willing to accept it. If she can see me, touch my hand, talk with me, the spell she is under may be broken.'

The idea had no appeal for him. He said crossly, 'You have been reading too many novels, and in any case you have not divined her character correctly. She is not simply a girl who feels herself wronged. There is something eccentric in her behaviour and in her attitude towards me. What kind of woman is it who tells lies about her lover to draw sympathy from others? I think she is out to ruin me and I do not want you to meet her.'

His words made her uneasy and she gave in without a struggle. 'Of course I will not if that is your wish.'

'It is, and please say nothing of this to my mother or to Célestine. I only hope that neither will become the recipient of army gossip.'

'Does *Maman* know of Mademoiselle Calvi's existence?' wondered Marie-Josèphe, curiosity overcoming her sense of delicacy.

Alain's look was only slightly reproving. '*Maman* is a realist. She knows my character and may have guessed that I am the sort of man who needs female companionship to balance against the horrors of war.'

'Indeed, I believe you are. But now, I urge you to put Mademoiselle Calvi out of your mind. She will eventually grow tired of making a nuisance of herself.'

'You are echoing the sentiments of Colonel Varesne.'

'Whom I have always regarded as a man endowed with more than his fair share of common sense.'

There the matter was allowed to rest, for Alain could not bring himself to tell Marie-Josèphe that a young lieutenant of the 4th Chasseurs à Cheval had picked a quarrel with him over Christina and had called him out. The duel was due to take place the following morning, which only went to show that the affair was becoming more ridiculous by the minute.

Alain hated everything to do with duelling, beginning with the foolish necessity of it. What did it matter if he had openly referred to Christina as a whore? It was what she was and the young lieutenant knew it. Why, then, the charade? Why the glint of outrage in the challenger's eye? No *lady's* honour had been impugned, no further harm done to a reputation already in shreds. He supposed this present business could be regarded as a tribute to Christina's mental sleight of hand, her ability to deceive the eye of a raw lieutenant by presenting him with the false image of a respectable, wronged woman who had been insultingly referred to as a whore. Abhorrent too were the rituals of duelling, the appointing of seconds and a referee, the choice of time, place and weapons, the false solemnity of it all.

Emil was of much the same mind. Alain's natural choice of second, he rode to the meeting, a deserted barn in a nearby village, grumbling most of the way about ungodly hours and stupid quarrels, and people who never learned to keep their mouths shut, until Alain felt obliged to ask him if he would prefer to change sides and represent Lieutenant Latouche. After due consideration Emil thought not, 'since Latouche is an even bigger fool than you are, old fellow.' The journey to the rendezvous was completed in aggrieved silence.

Lieutenant Latouche beat his rival to the rendezvous by a good ten minutes. Being but three weeks out of military academy and at his first posting, he had never smelt gunsmoke, nor yet drawn a sword in anger. He was pale and agitated and patently eager to begin the contest in defence of the indefensible.

'The word is that our friend is not much of a swordsman,' Emil murmured to Alain, 'so let him give you a scratch and then I will ask if he is satisfied.' He added with a knowing wink, 'My instinct tells me that he will be.'

'Oh, so I am to allow that frisking puppy over there to sink its teeth into me, am I?' complained Alain. 'That will do my reputation a great deal of good, I daresay.'

'To hell with your reputation,' Emil said, taking possession of the other's shako and cloak. 'The young man is so jumpy that if you lower your guard half a centimetre his sword will go straight through your gut and the Emperor will have lost a good cavalryman. What is more, His Imperial Majesty will spit on your corpse, figuratively speaking, that is. You know how he feels about duelling. He has declaimed his views on the subject often enough.'

'The last resort of the weak-minded who cannot settle their differences by rational argument. Yes, I know. Well, I am bound to admit that you are right about most things, my friend, so I will do as you say and let him walk on to me.'

But it was not to be so easy as that. The referee had no sooner given the signal for the contest to begin than the nervous challenger launched into a ferocious attack on his opponent which almost caught the latter off guard. Alain, finding himself very much on the defensive, had no recourse but to back off in order to give himself time to size up the situation. Latouche came after him like a tiger leaping on its prey, his sword slicing the air, his eyes round with menace and his teeth bared.

Alain worked hard to keep him at bay, but the other's very ineptness in the use of his weapon, the complete lack of co-ordination between hand and eye, made him very dangerous indeed. When Latouche's blade came within a centimetre of his right eye Alain decided that enough was enough. Swiftly, he deflected the stroke and forced the other's sword down on to his left wrist, where a cut opened up and a satisfying stream of blood ran down the back of his hand, dividing into channels between his fingers.

Emil, who had been waiting somewhat anxiously for this very occurrence, came running across the grass and placed himself between the two contestants. A crooked finger summoned the doctor, who earned his fee by declaring the wound to be nothing more than a scratch. The doctor's bored manner indicated his disgust at the idiocies of these young fighting cocks.

Latouche, who, in rule-book fashion, was standing rigidly to attention with his sword pointing downwards — the only correct move he had made that day — was addressed with grave formality by Emil. 'Are you satisfied?'

The young man hesitated. Emil lowered his voice. 'I would advise you to say yes, or your commanding officer may be interested to hear about a certain young officer falling asleep on guard duty. According to my informant the incident in question took place last Wednesday night.'

Seniority of service, combined with a touch of blackmail, rarely fails to make an impression. A stiff, slightly offended nod from Latouche and the farce was at an end.

'The young fool wanted to kill me,' Alain informed Emil as the two jogged their way back to Strasbourg. 'I could see it in his eyes, and all for the sake of a . . . '

'Stop! Do not say that word ever

again in connection with Christina,' warned his friend. 'Somehow or other that female has caught the popular fancy and is in danger of becoming fashionable. She is Beauty and you are the Beast, and the Beast had better retire to its lair to lick its wounds until this whole stupid affair is forgotten, otherwise it will almost certainly be attacked by some other young and eager gallant who wishes to defend the honour of a young lady of doubtful virtue.'

Alain was in no mood for theorizing. Glumly, he examined his damaged wrist. 'I must think of some plausible explanation to give to Marie-Josèphe as to why this scratch has all the appearance of a sword-cut.'

'Be sure to blow out the candle before you get into bed,' advised Emil.

8

From Jena to Friedland
1806 – 1807

It was autumn and the Emperor was planning a new campaign which bade fair to be a long one. France's enemies were gathering like the Assyrian hordes and at the next set-to there would be armies from Saxony, Russia, Sweden and Prussia all taking the field against their common foe.

Alain fell prey to a mixture of emotions as he checked his equipment and tested his horses for fitness. I may have been a father for several months by the time the fighting is over, he thought, and I shall not have laid eyes on my infant son or daughter. On the other side of the coin, he knew that he would be glad to get away from the hot-house atmosphere of a garrison town, where one's personal affairs were bandied about until one became the central figure in a *cause célèbre*. The duel with Latouche had caused quite a stir.

For the first time in his career Alain began to worry about getting killed. It was the price he had to pay for turning himself into a family man.

If Marie-Josèphe nursed a similar fear she gave no sign of it. The phrase 'When you return,' was frequently on her lips as she enumerated all the things she and Alain would do together with their new son/daughter. 'When you return,' said she, 'your connection with Mademoiselle Calvi will have been forgotten and she will have taken another lover. Indeed, she may already have done so. Elise told Emil that she is certain she saw her walking on the arm of Lieutenant Latouche.'

Alain kept his thoughts to himself. Marie-Josèphe was still blissfully ignorant of the fact that he had fought a duel with the champion of Christina's virtue.

The cut on his wrist had been noticed, but its origin not suspected.

The campaign, as anticipated, was to prove a lengthy operation which lasted from September, 1806 to July, 1807. Alain was at Marienberg in eastern Europe when he received a letter from his mother to say that Marie-Josèphe had borne him a son who was to be called Claude after his grandfather. 'The de Moissac line goes on,' the Countess had announced triumphantly.

Alain celebrated his paternity with Emil and a bottle of champagne. It was but a ritual performance; the fact was that he had become a father, but this seemed of little significance amidst the discomfort of long marches interspersed with short periods of oblivion in crowded quarters, or recumbent on the rain-soaked earth. He decided that he would have to see his son before he could begin to believe that he actually existed. Sometimes he even had to remind himself what his wife looked like by removing her miniature from his pocket and gazing sentimentally upon it.

Alain and Emil marched together and fought together all through the winter of 1806 – 7 and on into the spring and summer of 1807. They fought at Jena, Pultusk, Allenstein and Eylau, covering more than two thousand kilometres across eastern Europe and escaped with scarcely a scratch. Their luck ran out at Friedland on 14 June, 1807, where they were both severely wounded. Alain was hit by grape-shot — small lead balls contained in a canvas sack and propelled by a charge of gunpowder — in the fleshy part of his thigh and Emil received a wound, by the same means, behind his right knee. The latter's was by far the more serious injury.

Bandaged and still bleeding, Alain hobbled painfully the length of the field hospital looking for his friend. It took him twenty minutes to locate Emil among the closely packed ranks of stretchered men who waited for medical attention, some with quiet, uncomplaining patience, some begging for water, some petitioning heaven for mercy, for relief from intolerable pain, for temporary oblivion, even for death itself.

Alain, searching about him for hussar uniforms, found them and studied scores of ravaged faces until he encountered a pair of dark eyes, a large nose and the suggestion of a smile. Emil managed a feeble gesture with his right hand.

'Alain, thank God you are still alive. I saw you bowled over, old fellow, by the oddest looking creature in a billycock hat with a yellow feather in it. Are you badly hurt?'

Alain lowered himself carefully to the floor beside the prostrate figure. 'A chunk out of my backside. I shall not be able to sit down comfortably for quite a while. What about you?'

A wry grimace heralded disagreeable tidings. 'I have seen the surgeon and he says he will have to take off my right leg.'

The intelligence was received with a despairing groan. 'No! Oh, for God's sake, *no*!'

Emil seemed resigned to his fate. 'It is not uncommon for a soldier to lose a leg.'

'But are you sure that the leg cannot be saved?'

'How can I be sure of anything?' The wounded man spoke with the petulance of the dispirited invalid. 'I can only be guided by the surgeon.'

'It happens too often,' Alain grumbled. 'Do you know that? They do it to save time. A bad wound takes longer to heal than a cauterized stump.'

Emil closed his eyes. The sight of Alain's urgent expression induced total weariness. He said quietly, 'Well, I cannot see that it matters much. I have done my share to uphold the honour of France. I have killed quite a few of her enemies.'

'You call ten years' service upholding

the honour of France?' rejoined Alain unsympathetically. 'You have a lot left to do yet, my brave companion. Is your wound below the knee?'

'No, just above.'

'Where, exactly?'

The other stirred irritably. 'For Christ's sweet sake, I have just told you!'

'In front of the knee or behind?'

'Behind . . . now will you shut up?'

'The Emperor was wounded there once. He still has two legs.'

'He is the Emperor.'

'Imbecile. He was only a soldier when he was stuck with a pike by that English sergeant of dragoons . . . and besides, a crown does not make one less prone to injury than other men.'

Emil opened his eyes. 'Will you do something for me, Alain? Will you go away and lie down somewhere? Your wound is still bleeding. I can see the blood seeping through the bandage.'

Alain struggled to his feet. 'Anything to oblige. Your gratitude for my concern on your behalf overwhelms me, my friend. I will come back to see you later, when your mood is more mellow.'

So saying, he made off with as much speed as he could muster, for his own remark about the Emperor had given him an idea which in normal circumstances would have been still-born.

The harassed surgeon whom Alain now approached was Pasquale Pasiello, the very same who had patched him up at Austerlitz. He was extracting a bullet from the neck of a major of carabiniers. 'Surgeon,' began the interloper before his nerve failed him, 'one of my comrades-in-arms, Lieutenant Emil Durand by name, of the 7th Regiment of Hussars, is to have his leg amputated. Can you oblige me by telling me when that will be?'

Pasiello looked up briefly from his work, his eyes expressing the firm belief that his interrogater had gone stark mad, and answered grudgingly, 'How in the name of heaven do I know? He will take his turn with all the rest.'

'I imagine he will have to wait for quite a while, then?'

'At this rate, with a fool of a lieutenant pestering me, probably until Christmas!' roared Pasiello and applied himself more vigorously to his gory task. In doing so he dragged a faint moan from his groggy, brandy-soaked patient. 'Clear off, Lieutenant. You can see I am busy, I suppose? And if you must know, in this tent I take 'em according to rank — providing, of course, that they are not at death's door — and since there are two majors waiting to be sawn off, your comrade is not likely to be attended to just yet.'

With a muttered word of thanks Alain took his departure. Aware of a warm feeling in the vicinity of his left thigh, he looked down and saw that the bandage encircling the upper part of his leg was heavily stained. Hastily removing his red hussar's sash, he knotted it clumsily over the bandage.

For the moment at least he could no longer *see* himself bleeding, but what a sorry figure he must present with one leg of his breeches cut away and his bare, booted leg exposed to the common gaze!

Alain emerged from the field tent into a night of moonlight and stars and hailed a passing sergeant of dragoons, to whom he issued an order. A few minutes later the obliging veteran had assisted him to mount a tired grey and he was riding towards the village of Posthenen, which lay half a kilometre down the road. It was there that the Emperor had set up his headquarters in a vacated farmhouse.

The watch still ticking away in Alain's pocket registered one a.m., but despite the late hour the night was full of sounds. Men coughed and swore without venom, horses whickered and whinnied, camp-fires crackled and metal rasped against stone as swords were sharpened and cleaned in preparation for what the dawn might bring. For the French the battle was over and won, but enemies still lurked in the neighbourhood of the killing ground, waiting their chance to ambush the unwary victors. Victory was never that final. A small gathering of clouds raced across the moon, and the lone rider shivered in his torn uniform. He looked up into the sky and sensed that rain was on the way.

The farmhouse was swarming with members of the Emperor's staff. Alain slid off his horse and without ceremony accosted one of them more or less at random, although he was careful to pick upon a man who did not dramatically outrank him.

'Major, I must see His Majesty.'

The major, a man of thirty-five or thereabouts, spruce and un-battle-weary, eyed the intruder up and down. 'You are bleeding, Lieutenant.'

Alain forbore to follow the direction of the sharp, uncompassionate eyes and made no attempt to conceal his impatience. 'I am aware of that. I have come to see the Emperor.'

The other assumed the affronted expression of one who has been quite severely insulted. 'Name and regiment?'

'Lieutenant Alain d'Albert of the 7th Regiment of Hussars.'

'You have a message for the Emperor?'

'Yes.'

The major held out his hand. 'I will take it, if you please.'

Alain's leg was hurting like the fires of hell. He clung desperately to the remnants of his self-control. 'I was requested by my colonel to deliver the message in person. It is verbal.'

For some reason this seemed to amuse the major, who lowered his hand, gave a brief chuckle and enquired sharply, 'Why did not your commanding officer send someone sound in wind and limb?'

'Because I alone know the exact details of the incident which Colonel Varesne has instructed me to report, in person and without delay, to the Emperor.'

The major frowned and refused to budge. 'It is most irregular. I think you had better relay the message to me.'

It was with some relief that Alain discounted his own inferior status and allowed the anger to come out of him like a prolonged rush of wind. 'Dammit, Major, I am in no condition to sit down and write a report. I repeat, the message is verbal and while I am in the process of relaying it to you, I could very well bleed to death.'

A hard and challenging stare was directed at the obstacle in his path as he went on insultingly, 'If I report to my colonel that a major in a *clean* uniform prevailed upon me to countermand his orders and prevented me from carrying them out to the letter, he may not be too pleased, especially if I do bleed to death while I am standing listening to you being obstructive . . . sir.'

The slight contradiction contained in this statement appeared to elude the major's thinking processes. He caved in. It was the remark about the clean uniform that did it, the painful reminder that a temporarily crippling back injury had prevented his active participation in the campaign. Of course, this demented lieutenant could not know that, but if this Colonel Varesne chose to make a fuss and the Emperor got to hear that he, Major Maret, had delayed communication to him of some intelligence of an important nature, there could be hell to pay, depending on what sort of mood His Imperial Majesty was in at the time. In wartime, the major reminded himself, protocol often went by the board. 'Follow me!' he snapped.

The Emperor had commandeered the whole of a sizeable farmhouse, the occupants of which had been relegated to the doubtful comforts of their own barn; dire threats were muttered against the Corsican usurper to an assortment of surprised animals.

His Majesty was presently in occupation of the *petit salon*. Alain, entering the farmhouse through the front door behind his disgruntled conductor, became instantly aware of breasting his way through a sea of uniforms which, beginning at the door with the insignia of an assortment of captains and majors, ranked ever higher as he drew nearer to the seat of power. He was also uncomfortably conscious of a number of curious glances being directed at his generally dishevelled appearance and at the knotted sash adorning his leg.

Alain kept his eyes firmly fixed on the small of the major's back and dogged his heels until a large mahogany table, at which a man sat eating a meagre meal, obstructed further progress. The man's pale, tired-looking features brooded over his plate while his hand, holding a silver fork engraved with the imperial arms, toyed with a piece of meat which was pushed slowly round the plate in an anti-clockwise direction, completing two circuits before it was transferred to his rather small mouth. After this languid performance the fork was deposited on the plate and the plate pushed away almost petulantly, as if the diner was bored with the business of eating.

It was only when the major bowed reverentially that Alain realised he had at last reached the fountain-head. During the whole of his military service he had never had an opportunity of observing the Emperor at really close quarters and without his hat. Hastily and clumsily he followed the major's lead. When he straightened up his immediate impression was of jet-black, slightly receding hair, grey, penetrating eyes and the blue, gold-braided uniform of a *général en chef*.

The Emperor looked Alain up and down, noted the evidence of a wound and turned his gaze enquiringly upon the major. The latter leaned towards him and in subdued tones explained the substance of Alain's request. Alain caught the words 'a little battle-crazed,' and bridled instantly under the insult.

The mesmeric eyes saw and registered interest.

'You have a message for me, Lieutenant?'

Now that he had got past the first — some would say the insuperable obstacle — Alain was somewhat at a loss as to how to go on. He became hesitant and groped for words. 'Your Majesty, I . . . I . . .' and as the eyes hardened with a nameless suspicion, the suspicion of one who has had several attempts made on his life, 'It is my friend, Your Majesty, Lieutenant Emil Durand. The surgeon wants to take off his leg, but . . .'

At this juncture Major Maret, with all his worst fears about this presumptuous junior officer confirmed, allowed his indignation to burst out of him like pus from a boil. 'Lieutenant! You told me you had a message, sanctioned by your colonel, to deliver to His Majesty. This is rank insubordination . . . deception . . . a court-martial offence!'

If a man could ever be said to froth

at the mouth Major Maret did then. A small trickle of saliva dribbled down his chin.

'Major Maret!' The measured voice of the Emperor cut across the vehement protests and the steady gaze fastened itself upon Alain's face. 'Go on, Lieutenant.'

A wave of pure relief swept over Alain. He was going to get a hearing. 'Your Majesty, Durand and I have fought together since 1797. We had the honour of serving Your Majesty in Italy, at Marengo and at Austerlitz, and we have done our part this day in securing Your Majesty's great victory. We are like brothers, Durand and I. Now my friend has a wound in his leg which the surgeon declares will not heal. He says the leg must come off, but I am of the contrary opinion, although I must confess that I have not actually seen the wound. In spite of that I am sure the possibility exists that the leg could be saved.'

The major was still on the boil. 'And

what makes you think, Lieutenant, that your contrary opinion can have the least value against that of a regimental surgeon? By your own admission you have not actually seen Durand's wound and therefore cannot, in honesty, presume to give an opinion upon it.'

A faint twitch of amusement could be discerned tugging at the corners of the imperial mouth. The eyes indicated that an answer was required.

Not deigning to spare the major so much as a glance, Alain addressed the one man who had the power to help him. 'Because, Your Majesty, my friend, who is certainly in the best position to know, described to me the exact location of the injury and from that description I deduced the fact that it is similar to that which Your Majesty sustained in the year 1793. I remember hearing it said that Your Majesty would on no account permit a surgeon to amputate the limb. At the time Your Majesty was a young man, holding the rank of major in the Royal Artillery, with insufficient medical knowledge to dispute the decision of a surgeon, but Your Majesty had the courage to defy his opinion and . . . '

Alain broke off, confused, as the Emperor's staff closed in about him, openly aghast at this intrusive lieutenant who was spinning some tale about a wounded comrade and reminding the Emperor of his humble beginnings to boot.

Alain concluded feebly, 'I beg Your Majesty's pardon for deceiving Major Maret. There was no message. I came here to plead on behalf of my friend, who hopes that his two legs will continue to serve Your Majesty for as long as it is Your Majesty's pleasure to command them.'

The entourage waited breathlessly for imperial rage to burst like a thundercloud and reduce Lieutenant d'Albert to a sodden mess. They waited in vain. 'What do you want *me* to do?'

Alain inhaled deeply. 'I would beg Your Majesty to come and look at my friend's wound and give your opinion as to whether or not his leg should be taken off.'

Concerted gasps of shock and disbelief from marshals, generals and aides greeted this presumptuous request. The Emperor ignored the tumult, rose from the table and enquired of no one in particular, 'Where is Larrey?'

Surgeon Dominique Jean Larrey, soon to become Baron Larrey, a mark of distinction for his outstanding abilities as a physician, was Senior Medical Officer of the *Grande Armée*.

'Fetch him!' came the curt command, and to Alain, 'Well, Lieutenant, let us be off. Take me to see your valued friend.'

There was a scramble for the door and a rising babble of sound. Alain allowed himself to be hustled along, noting as he did so that he had actually rubbed shoulders with Marshal Lannes, looking thin and ill as a result of his exertions over the last nine months.

To say that the Emperor caused a mild sensation as he strode into the field hospital would be something of an understatement. Medical orderlies snapped to attention and the wounded who were in full possession of their senses seemed, if such a thing were possible, to come to attention lying down, sprawled bodies elongating into slender, straight lines.

Pasiello, who was still occupied with his grisly work, flicked his important visitor a startled glance and went on sawing away at the leg of a captain of carabiniers, who was being held down by an obliging, and presumably egalitarian, *Chef de Brigade*.

The hangers-on were now banished with a brief imperial command and there remained only the Emperor, Surgeon Larrey, Alain and a few medical orderlies standing amidst the dead and dying. Emil confessed afterwards to Alain that when he saw the Emperor approaching his pallet he nearly died of shock, which would have been a sad end to the whole affair, but that he managed to rally 'at the sight of you, old fellow, leading the way and limping along in front of His Majesty like the last survivor of the seven legions of Marcus Crassus.'

The Emperor acknowledged the dumbfounded patient with a friendly nod and turning to Larrey, whose rough-hewn features showed not the least surprise at his master's actions, said, 'Take a look, will you, Larrey, and give me your opinion on this man's wound, then I will give you mine. It is to be hoped that we shall be in agreement.'

Larrey pulled away the rough woollen blanket from Emil's recumbent form and taking a knife from his pocket, cut away the torn breeches from the shattered leg, an operation which he performed with difficulty, since the material was stuck by coagulated blood to the flesh. Emil went very white but made no sound. The Emperor stroked his forehead in an oddly tender gesture.

'It has not even been looked at,' he murmured to Larrey, 'so how the devil did the surgeon come to the conclusion that the leg should be taken off?'

Larrey shot him an expressive look and shrugged as if to say, 'It would be better for Your Majesty not to enquire too closely into that.'

The exposed wound was about twelve centimetres long and so deep that a small section of bone showed whitely through. Larrey inspected the mangled flesh thoughtfully and at considerable length. The Emperor, who was peering over his shoulder, grew impatient.

'It will heal,' he declared confidently. 'It is no worse than mine was.' He turned to speak to Alain. 'Very astute of you, young man, to act upon your own gut feeling. Durand is fortunate to have you for a friend.'

Larrey said sourly, 'I perceive that

176

Your Majesty does not require me to render my professional opinion.'

'But you will give it all the same.'

Larrey looked grimly amused. 'So I shall. It is this. The leg *may* heal. Amputation *may* not be necessary.'

'Good. Convey my compliments to the surgeon who is in charge here and give him my orders to the effect that Lieutenant Durand is not to have his leg amputated at present.'

Once more he turned to Alain. 'The name of the surgeon, Lieutenant. Do you know it?'

Alain, who could hardly conceal his joy at Emil's reprieve, answered at once, 'He is Dr. Pasquale Pasiello, Your Majesty.'

'Ah!' The Emperor nodded as if to say, 'I know the breed well.' Aloud he said, 'An Italian. He is bound to be touchy if his judgment is questioned, even if that judgment is based on nothing more solid than a cursory glance at a man lying flat on his back and covered with a blanket.'

He swung back to face Larrey. 'I therefore urge you to be tactful, my friend. That particular virtue is not your strong point, I know, but do your best.'

Larrey would dearly have loved to reply, 'Nor, I believe, can Your Majesty lay claim to it,' but desisted. He had been caustic enough for one day.

Alain opened his mouth to express his humble and heartfelt thanks, and to declare his everlasting devotion to the Emperor, but a wave of nausea swept over him, darkness closed in behind a cloud of fog and he dropped like a stone.

Faintness dissolved into the sleep of exhaustion and when Alain came to he was stretched out on a straw pallet in the field hospital with his leg neatly bandaged. On the next pallet lay Emil. Still in possession of both legs, he was sound asleep and snoring off the effects of twelve drops of laudanum.

★ ★ ★

Alain was up and about in three days and Emil in ten. The latter expressed his gratitude to his friend by providing him with a new horse, Roland having given up his life for France at the battle of Friedland. Alain was too polite to ask Emil how he got the white stallion, but he could not help noticing that the harness and bridle with which the animal was equipped were stamped with the double-headed imperial eagle of Austria. The spoils of war.

The details of Lieutenant d'Albert's exploit on behalf of his friend had run round the regiment like wildfire and Alain discovered that he had become something of a celebrity. Fellow-officers came up to him and clapped him on the shoulder, offering remarks such as, 'Congratulations, my friend. Me, I should not have had the nerve,' or 'I hear that the English want to give you a medal for bravery in face of the enemy.'

Alain took it all in his stride, knowing

that within a week the incident would have conceded first place to another, more immediately interesting, item of news.

Letters arrived from Strasbourg, one a scrawled missive from Elise professing undying love for Emil — at which the object of her passion gave a loud, derisive laugh — and would he bring her back a shawl? And another from Marie-Josèphe with, among all the family news which included the interesting fact that Célestine had a suitor, a truly astounding message.

'Mademoiselle Calvi,' wrote Marie-Josèphe, 'is now Madame Georges Batut, Madame *Général* Georges Batut. She outranks us, my dear! How I should love to be with you to see your face the instant you read these words. It came about thus: Mademoiselle Calvi, after playing out her little charade of dogging your heels through Strasbourg and beyond, must have decided that you were lost to her for ever and placed herself under the protection of Lieutenant Latouche, your duelling opponent. Oh, yes, my darling, I now know all about that sordid affair. Did you really imagine that the female gossips of Strasbourg would allow me to remain for ever in ignorance of the fact that my husband had been fighting a duel over his former mistress, albeit unwillingly, I am reliably informed? What an *éclat* over the tea-cups! I feel compelled to warn you that from now on you had better mind your language when you refer to Madame Batut. She is most certainly not to be referred to as a whore . . . '

Alain groaned resignedly before reading on: 'Lieutenant Latouche, as I expect you know, is the nephew of General Batut. The unfortunate young man took Mademoiselle Calvi, as she then was, to the opera and introduced her to his uncle as his future wife. This seems to have been rather a bad mistake on his part because the General was so overwhelmed by Mademoiselle Calvi's charms that he quite forgot he was to be the bride's uncle and adopted the rôle of bridegroom instead, much to the discomfiture of his nephew. The marriage took place in Strasbourg about a month after you left and just three days before the general got on his horse and tagged along after the rest of you. Now I come to the sad part. Lieutenant Latouche was killed at Jena, in case you had not heard. Some of us poor mortals are cruelly treated by fate, do you not agree?'

Alain read out the relevant part of his wife's letter to Emil, who showed great appreciation of Marie-Josèphe's wry sense of humour. 'So, Christina has attained respectability at last,' he said. 'You may invite her to your house now, Alain, that is if she will condescend to pass through your portals.'

Alain laughed. 'I think any further intercourse between Madame Batut and the d'Albert family must surely be at an end.'

Following the battle of Friedland the Emperor of France met the Emperor of

Russia at Tilsit, or more precisely on a raft moored in the middle of the river Niemen, and together they hammered out peace terms, reversing alliances and juggling with frontiers as if they were playing some gigantic game of chess. Alexander professed himself enchanted with his brother-emperor and fellow-soldier. In the sphere of warfare the Russian Emperor was a novice sitting at the feet of the master, and like the immature boy he was he reaped a harvest of meaningless *bons mots* which fell from the lips of one much noted for such pearls of wisdom. 'The secret of success is to be afraid last,' was a sentiment which particularly appealed to him.

So there was to be peace for a time until the vacillating Alexander lent an ear to the enemies of Napoleon Bonaparte and once more plunged Europe into war.

9

Strasbourg
1807

August in Strasbourg was hot and steamy. It was a time for post-campaign parties and receptions, a time for returning heroes to relax in the company of wives and mistresses, a time for widows to mourn and a time for young lieutenants to receive their promotions. Alain and Emil were promoted to captaincies at the end of September.

Célestine d'Albert had given her susceptible heart to a major of the de Chamborant regiment and it only wanted Alain's approval to the match for her happiness to be complete. Alain knew Major Fels, an old campaigner like himself, and gave it without demur. The wedding was quickly arranged, for the times were uncertain and happiness, like all other fleeting conditions, must be taken at the flood. Célestine was dowered with money which had come via Monsieur Cabarroques, confectioner to the Empress Josephine. How satisfactorily things were working out for the d'Albert family. The bride went to live in a small house in the Rue St. Martin with her new husband.

In November of that same year Alain and Marie-Josèphe received an invitation to attend a regimental ball which was to be held in the house of Général and Madame Batut in the Rue Roi-Soleil. The ball was in the nature of a belated celebration of the Général's marriage, all festivities having been postponed by the demands of war. It was also the general's way of thanking his junior officers for a job well done.

The d'Albert family were at afternoon tea when the invitation arrived and was brought to Alain by a servant who, while presenting the silver tray on which reposed a white, gold-embossed card, obligingly removed the master's nine-month-old son from his lap and deposited the child on the floor. Claude d'Albert, accepting his rejection with placid good humour, set off in a fast crawl towards his mother.

Alain examined the card and read the words inscribed upon it with a start of surprise. 'Good God!'

The mild expletive drew expectant glances from his wife and mother who were curious to know what had occasioned it. Alain's first instinct had been to shove the card into his pocket for later consideration, but his exclamation had betrayed his surprise and with two pairs of demanding female eyes upon him this was clearly not a practical course of action. The truth must out.

He said, 'We are all invited to a ball on Wednesday next at the home of General Batut.'

The Countess, who by now knew every last detail of her son's liaison with the new Madame Batut, declared emphatically, 'We shall refuse, of course.'

Alain fingered his upper lip, where a newly-grown moustache — neither obligatory nor forbidden for a hussar — was sprouting nicely and had prompted a remark from Marie-Josèphe to the effect that he now looked 'horribly villainous.'

'I do not see how I can possibly refuse, *Maman*. An invitation from a Général is more in the nature of a command.'

'Have you considered the feelings of Marie-Josèphe?'

The Countess was very fond of her daughter-in-law and deeply regretted that her son's connection with a soldier's woman had come to light. The damage had been done, but the fact that Marie-Josèphe had examined the matter in her usual sensible fashion did not mean that she should be placed in a position where she would have to exchange pleasantries with her husband's paramour.

An expression of horror crossed her face. 'Surely the general can know nothing of the duel which took place between you and his nephew, Alain? And pray do not glare at Marie-Josèphe in that disgusting fashion. I learned of your piece of foolishness not from my daughter-in-law, but from some of the ladies, or so they call themselves, of this talkative garrison town. I believe you used a most derogatory term in relation to Madame Batut which gave Lieutenant Latouche a reason for calling you out. Can you believe that the general, knowing this, would invite you to his house, and can you bring yourself to go under a cloak of deceit?'

Alain tossed the invitation onto a nearby table. 'Whether he knows or not, *Maman*, is immaterial. He has invited us and I think we should go. You may be interested to know that Général Batut does not spring from the first order of society. His father was a tradesman and as a young man, before he joined the army, Batut worked as a shop assistant. In other words, he cannot be classed as a gentleman. If he knows of my insulting reference to his wife it may be that he does not regard it as a matter of consequence.'

'My dear Alain, you test my credulity to the limit,' returned his mother, cutting a piece of sponge-cake into three precisely measured slices. 'Are you asking me to believe that your very pleasant friend, Emil Durand, whose father is a tailor, a fact which he conveyed to me with his usual charmingly unreserved frankness, would not shun you for ever were you to refer to a female member of his family in such terms?'

'Emil is a natural gentleman,' rejoined Alain. 'The general, I fear, is not. He says what he thinks with complete disregard for the social conventions and spends a great deal of time insulting ladies himself without realising he is doing it. He once referred to the wife of Captain Bessières, in public, as 'fatter than a pregnant mare.' The only reason that the captain did not call him out is because he is astute enough to realise that the general is too dull-witted to know that his words might be taken as a personal slur on the lady in question.'

'And because the general outranks him,' put in Marie-Josèphe. 'Is it not forbidden for officers of dissimilar ranks to call each other out?'

Alain gave a grim chuckle. 'I rather think a little thing like rank would not have stopped the captain had he thought the quarry worth pursuing.'

'All of which gets us nowhere,' said the Countess. 'Do you mean to go to the general's ball or not?'

Marie-Josèphe was feeding her son bread and butter. The child accepted the dull fare obediently and with one envious eye on his grandmother's sponge-cake. His mother bubbled over with laughter. 'Eat this and you shall have some cake, greedy-one,' she promised.

Alain gazed fondly at the charming tableau and offered generously, 'I will send my regrets to the general if you would rather not go, my dearest. Even generals can be placated with a convincing excuse of indisposition.'

Marie-Josèphe shook her head decisively. 'As usual, you and I, Captain, are in perfect accord. I too think we should go. Who knows? Perhaps Madame Batut is anxious to make up for the embarrassment she caused us earlier this year. I have always felt that she was more to be pitied than condemned.'

'You are too forgiving, my dear,' said her mother-in-law. 'Madame Batut's actions, if not activated by malice, were at best the work of a devious and stubborn woman.' A defiant look was directed at Alain. 'For my part, I intend to plead an indisposition. Ladies of mature years like myself are prone to headaches, especially in November.'

By tacit consent no more was said on the vexed subject and Alain was relieved that he would not have to offer some paltry excuse for the non-attendance of Marie-Josèphe and himself at the general's ball.

The Hotel de Montpensier, home of Général and Madame Batut, was split up into four separate apartments, one of which was leased by the general on a short-term basis. On the night of the ball three rooms had been opened up in *enfilade*, one as an improvised ballroom, one as a buffet-hall and the third as a drawing-room for older guests, who wished only to sit and talk; exhausted dancers would gather there at the end of the evening. In all three rooms crystal chandeliers cast their radiance on an abundance of gilded wood and red plush and warmed the revellers into the bargain.

In the ante-chamber to the makeshift ballroom Général and Madame Batut waited to receive their guests, who were being announced by a flunkey in white silk breeches and a blue cut-away tail-coat.

'How grand!' murmured Marie-Josèphe. She clung to the arm of her husband as the line of guests moved slowly forward. The general was fat, bald and blind in one eye, the first two afflictions being entirely attributable to the work of nature and the last to a piece of shrapnel which had lodged in his right eye at the battle of Austerlitz. If he knew of Alain's former liaison with his wife he gave no sign of it as he acknowledged the other's respectful bow, then raised Marie-Josèphe's hand to his lips.

The single, rather protruding brown eye returned immediately to Alain. 'I should be obliged, Captain, if you would come to my private room after I have finished receiving. Bernard will show you the way.' He indicated the flunkey in the blue tail-coat by stabbing a thick forefinger at the individual in question.

Unfeignedly surprised by this invitation, Alain murmured assent and moved on to pay his respects to

Christina, who was looking extremely elegant in a low, off-the-shoulder gown of white silk decorated with lilac bows and appliqué-work. A silk turban, ornamented with lilac plumes and ropes of pearls, covered her dark hair and a painted silk fan dangled from her wrist. Her heelless slippers were of white satin, laced across the instep.

Not that Alain noticed all this, except perhaps the lilac plumes which seemed to have a life of their own as they swayed gently to and fro before his bemused eyes. The ensemble is described simply to give the reader some idea of what the fashionable French lady of 1807 was wearing.

'Madame Batut.' Alain tried to instil some warmth into the salutation, but memories of the past were too vivid and prevented more than a tepid smile and the feeblest of handshakes.

'Captain d'Albert.' She looked genuinely pleased to see him. 'Permit me to congratulate you on your promotion. I am so happy that you could come.'

He had to hand it to her. She was playing the *grande dame* as well as if she had been born to the rôle. He should have been amused by her performance and wondered why he only felt irritated.

Christina's eyes transferred themselves to Marie-Josèphe and the two women touched hands. No further words were exchanged before the general's lady turned her attention to the next arrivals.

Alain hurried Marie-Josèphe on into the ballroom, where the dancing had already commenced. 'The old boy wants to see me after he has finished receiving,' he whispered into her ear. 'Did you hear?'

She nodded affirmatively.

'Will you wait for me in the drawing-room, or shall I ask Emil to look after you?'

'I will go with Emil,' she decided at once. 'The drawing-room is sure to be full of older ladies wanting to know if I am with child. They seem to think that it is the only proper condition for a young matron like myself to be in.'

She looked up at Alain, her expression serious and thoughtful. 'What do you suppose the general wants to talk to you about?'

He shrugged. 'Who knows? Something to do with the recent campaign, perhaps . . . and stop looking so worried. I assure you that I am not about to be called out for once having known the general's wife.'

The general's study-cum-office was littered with maps and books and discarded jackets and boots; the aura of masculinity abounded. As Alain insinuated himself into this organised chaos the man he had come to see was to be discovered seated at his desk quaffing a large glass of brandy and loosening his uniform collar, simultaneous acts which suggested that he was in need of some therapeutic activity now that the irksome business of receiving, so foreign to his nature, was over. The visitor was waved to a chair.

'No ceremony, Captain. Social occasion. Tonight you are my house guest. Not on parade.'

The general spoke loudly and distinctly and in short bursts, which probably accounted for the fact that the men under his command were in the habit of referring to him irreverently as 'old grape-shot.' His strange manner of speech, an affectation 'caught' from a superior officer when the general was a mere captain, had one distinct advantage. It made it extremely easy to catch the speaker's drift.

'Brandy, Captain?'

'I am much obliged to you, sir.'

A large and brimming glass was accepted with some misgivings as Alain waited uneasily for what was to come. Despite his confident assurances to Marie-Josèphe, he was not altogether convinced that a reference to his youthful philanderings was entirely out of the question.

He need not have worried. The general leaned back in his chair and barked, 'I have spoken to Colonel Varesne about you, Captain. Want you to become my aide-de-camp. Admired the way you approached the Emperor about your friend. Not orthodox, mind you. Not to be recommended on every occasion, but I understand your motives. Had a desire to come face to face with the great one, no doubt. Wanted to speak to him, man to man, catch some of the glory, eh?'

There was a silence as vast as the Siberian wastes before Alain replied, 'My sole motive in approaching the Emperor was a resolve to do everything possible to save my friend's leg, sir. The surgeons work their saws too vigorously by half when they are hard-pressed.'

A single speculative eye was directed at Alain as the general took a quick swallow of his brandy. 'Yes, well, it showed initiative anyway, and that is what I like to have about me, men with initiative. You will take the job?'

'May I crave the general's indulgence and ask for time to think it over?'

The old veteran frowned into his empty brandy glass. 'That is a damned peculiar request, Captain. What is to think over when you are offered promotion? You are a married man, right? With a child? Yes? More to come if nature has her way. Done your share, according to my informants. Wounded at Austerlitz and Friedland. Time your wife had a say, what? She would rather have a live husband than a dead hero, I daresay.'

Alain had drained his glass rather too quickly. The effect of a rush of alcohol to the brain made him bold. 'The battlefields of Europe have been littered with dead aides, sir.'

'True,' conceded the general, shifting his ground and refilling his glass at the same time. 'To be honest, I have lost one or two myself.' The eye was directed thoughtfully at the ceiling.

'One fell at Montebello, if I remember rightly, another at Austerlitz, two at Jena . . . by heaven, yes, two at Jena . . . Careless of them, I thought. One rode right in front of an oncoming cavalry charge and got mowed down . . . damned nuisance that because he was bringing me intelligence of an important nature and it got delayed, and the other . . . now what happened to him? Oh, yes, that was at Eylau . . . he had his horse shot under him and fetched up in the path of a cannon ball.'

The eye was lowered and brought to bear once more on Alain. 'That makes four, yes? The fifth went at Friedland. I was fond of him, poor devil. Garat was his name, Captain Louis Garat. Dashing sort of fellow. Game for anything. Reminded me of myself at his age. Got shot in the chest by a musket ball. Accident, of course. Those things are never accurate more than a few centimetres off target. Have some more brandy, Captain?'

The bottle was pushed invitingly towards Alain. He stared at it doubtfully, was tempted and declined. Marie-Josèphe detested insobriety. She called it a desertion of the mind.

Having entirely demolished his original line of argument concerning the indestructibility of aides, the general re-adopted it with a bland insouciance which had Alain mentally gasping.

'Not so much chance of getting killed when you are running about with messages, is there? What say, Captain? A softer bed to lie on before you step up the next rung of the ladder, or put yourself out to pasture? Do you mean to stay in the army? Make it a career for life?'

The barrage of questions left Alain looking bewildered and caused him to answer uncertainly, 'I cannot say, sir. It is the only life I know.'

'Best to stick with it while you are sound in wind and limb then,' advised the general. 'In my view a life of retirement is for the cripples, but hellish boring for the rest of us. Agree with me, do you?'

'Yes, sir.'

'Fancy yourself as a marshal of France?'

The suggestion brought a smile. 'I would not quite aspire to becoming a marshal, sir, but if one's capabilities match one's ambitions I suppose there is no harm in wishing for higher things.'

'To be up there with the Emperor. Yes, as you say, Captain, there is no harm in wishing. It is settled then, is it? You agree to become my aide?'

'If you think I am up to the job, sir,' responded Alain weakly and wondered whether his surrender had been occasioned by the general's forceful methods of persuasion, or whether it had been the natural consequence of imbibing rather more brandy than was his custom.

Marie-Josèphe and Emil were dancing a minuet together when Alain reappeared in the ballroom. He stood watching them for a moment, his eye enchanted by their stately progress and by the grace with which his wife moved. Seconds later Emil observed the observer and whispered something to his partner. The couple left the set to join Alain and all three passed on into the buffet-hall, where Marie-Josèphe was immediately accosted by a female acquaintance. With a comical look over her shoulder at her husband she allowed herself to be borne away.

As the two men drifted towards the tempting array of food set out on the tables amidst arrangements of flowers and gleaming silver cutlery, Alain told Emil what had passed between himself and the general.

'Congratulations.' His friend's glance was quizzical. 'Is it what you wanted, old fellow?'

Still looking a little dazed from his recent encounter, Alain replied, 'To be frank, I have not yet had time to examine my thoughts on the subject. It is a step up, to be sure.'

Emil, fork in hand, began spearing slices of ham on to a plate, together with a considerable quantity of other comestibles. 'Running round after the ladies?'

Alain bridled. 'What the hell do you mean?'

Emil roared with laughter at the sight of the other's indignant expression. 'Well, not on campaign, I grant you, but here in garrison you will be for ever on the trot. I have heard it said that one of Général Victor's aides shops for his wife's cap ribbons and lace collars.'

'You made that up!'

'No, really, on my honour it is true.' Emil leaned confidentially towards Alain. 'It is even rumoured that he has learned to sew.'

A black scowl warned the persecutor of newly-appointed aides to change the subject, which he did, picking on one hardly less controversial. 'What will Marie-Josèphe think when she finds out that you are to come into almost daily contact with Christina?'

'Nothing, I hope.' Alain was making a difficult choice between chicken and veal pie and smoked salmon. 'She has more sense than to suspect me of rekindling that old fire.'

'That confident, are you?'

Alain forked up a piece of smoked salmon and turned to face Emil. 'What are you suggesting?'

The dark eyes of the other expressed mild concern. 'Only that you are still somewhat naïve about the inner workings of the female mind, old fellow. I meant no offence.'

'You appear to be implying that Marie-Josèphe may have some doubts concerning my fidelity towards her.'

'Nothing of the kind, but she may have some doubts concerning Christina's willingness to bury the past. She may even think that Christina engineered your appointment as her husband's aide.'

Alain mumbled through a mouthful of food, 'It is not possible. Christina would not carry that amount of influence.'

'I would not bet on it, old fellow. Christina was always very persuasive, and we must not forget that she beds with the general. A hell of a lot of bargains are struck between a man and a woman thrashing about on top of a feather mattress. I would not mind betting that the course of history has been changed as the result of a woman haggling with a man under a counterpane.'

These words disturbed Alain more than he cared to admit. 'Always supposing I accept your hypothesis,' said he, 'what would be her motive in doing such a thing? Some weird kind of revenge because I would not marry her? An attempt to resume our former relationship?'

Emil pulled a face. 'Do not ask me to read the mind of a woman. I gave up that sort of thing years ago. I will tell you this, though. If Christina had been my woman, I should have got rid of her the moment she started behaving towards me like a wife.'

Alain nodded gloomily. 'Do you think I should tell the general that I have changed my mind about becoming his aide?'

'Not at all. That would be breaking your word and would do your reputation little good. My advice to you is to proceed with caution, and if Christina looks as if she is about to ambush you, beat a retreat. In other words, employ sound military tactics in all your future dealings with the lady.'

'I am obliged to you for your *sound* advice,' replied Alain with heavy irony. 'I only hope I can spot the ambush before the enemy leaps out and sets upon me.'

'The time to watch for an ambush is when you are reasonably confident that there is not going to be one,' chuckled Emil and was just about to engorge a sizeable slice of fruit cake when his expression changed and he looked about him with that air of desperation which a sniper is wont to display when he has left his flank unprotected.

'I think you may soon be sent about your first errand, old fellow,' he whispered urgently. 'Christina is approaching us wearing her purposeful look, so I will say *au revoir*.'

With a shrug and an apologetic grin, Emil, still clutching his piece of cake, backed away from Alain and melted into the press of military uniforms clustered about the laden tables.

'Coward!' Alain mouthed at his departing back and turned like an animal at bay to face the threat of a determined woman. Out of the corner of his eye he saw Marie-Josèphe deep in conversation with Madame Varesne and longed to join her, but he was already too late.

She came towards him smiling. 'Captain d'Albert. I am so glad to learn that you have decided to accept my husband's offer,' were her first words. 'He badly needs someone upon whom he can depend.' A light laugh accompanied her next remark. 'His last aide, who was killed at Friedland, was always chasing girls, poor man.'

She took a step nearer to him and lowered her voice. 'Alain, I hope the past is forgotten? We both have new lives to lead now.'

He eyed her warily. Christina had always been good at mimicking sincerity. 'Was it at your suggestion that General Batut decided to appoint me to his staff?'

She looked him straight in the eye. 'How could you think that? It is not my business to influence appointments. Alain, I am happily married. I have put all girlish foolishness behind me.'

He did not know whether to believe her but thought that an apology was in order. 'I am sorry. I just thought . . . I mean I thought that you might . . . ' He broke off in confusion.

'That I might still be in love with you?'

'Well, yes, I . . . ' He remembered that he was speaking to the wife of his superior officer and finished firmly, 'It was impertinent of me. I apologise unreservedly.'

She regarded him for a long moment with that vague, withdrawn expression he knew so well, but had never been able to interpret. Then she said, 'I still have a high regard for you, Alain.'

He acknowledged this statement with the suggestion of a bow.

'I should like to think that I still merit your regard.'

'Naturally.'

He felt awkward in her presence and wished she would go away to talk to somebody else. A sidelong glance to his left revealed the fact that Marie-Josèphe was an interested spectator of his meeting with Madame Batut. Christina, following the direction of his eyes, saw her too and complimented her rival. 'Your wife is very beautiful.'

'Yes, she is.'

'I know that you have always been an admirer of beautiful women and I have often wondered, therefore, why you chose me to be your mistress, since I could never lay claim to good looks. What was it about me that you admired, Alain?'

His frown bordered on severity. 'You really cannot expect me to answer that. Now, if you will excuse me, Madame, my wife is waiting for me. I promised to partner her in the gavotte.'

Her eyes held him rooted to the spot. 'They are still playing a coranto and it is uncivil of you to evade answering my question.'

'Forgive me, but you must not expect a soldier to remember everything about the women he has slept with.'

'I had forgotten how cruel you could be.'

For one awful moment he thought she was about to burst into tears and hastened to forestall the possibility of an embarrassing public outburst. 'For God's sake, Christina, but a moment since you were telling me that you were happily married and that your passion for me had given way to a high regard.

Am I now to assume that you were not telling me the truth? If your attitude towards me is to be one of repining I shall be forced to decline the general's offer, much as it will grieve me to make myself look a complete fool.'

'No.' She laid her hand on his arm. 'I meant what I said about being happily married. It was silly and vain of me to ask such a question. It is never wise to look back, is it?'

'No.'

'If it will set your mind at rest, I must tell you that my husband, if he knows of it, has never made any reference to my previous association with you. He knows, of course, that I am a woman with a past, but his love for me overcame any scruples he might have had in that respect. I lived for a time with his nephew. You know that, I expect?'

'Yes.'

'Lieutenant Latouche, he with whom you fought the duel.'

'I remember him well.'

'Latouche said that you referred to me in insulting terms.'

'I called you a soldier's woman.'

'You called me a whore.'

'It is more or less the same thing, and how gallant of your brave lieutenant to repeat my words to you.'

'He was rather a stupid young man.'

'But you have reason to be grateful to him, since he introduced you to his uncle.'

She side-stepped this obvious truth. 'He was killed at the battle of Jena.'

'Latouche, you mean. Yes, so I believe.'

The pointless exchange was getting on his nerves. What obscure message was she trying to convey? He brought it to an abrupt and discourteous end by the simple expedient of walking away. '*Au revoir*, Madame.'

She made no protest, but he was aware that her eyes followed him as he rejoined his wife.

'Madame Batut seemed to have plenty to say,' remarked Marie-Josèphe, as husband and wife made their way to the ballroom.

'Christina always had plenty to say,' replied Alain. 'Verbosity is one of the less attractive facets of her nature.'

'Emil told me your news.'

'Oh?' He sounded glum.

'Are you not flattered to be noticed by a general?'

'I would be if he were a man of intellect. Unfortunately, he is a man of coarse habits and little education.'

'But he must be a good soldier to have risen to the rank of general.'

'I cannot dispute that. He has the reputation of being a brilliant tactician and he cares about the welfare of his men. He has been known to weep over the dead and wounded, a weakness which would be regarded with suspicion, when coupled with the fact that he can get through a bottle of brandy a day.'

'I really do not like you very much when you are being cynical,' declared Marie-Josèphe.

'Your accusation is unjust. If you had heard, as I did, Batut discussing the demise of five of his aides in the most callous terms, you would not have made it.'

With her usual easy good humour she changed the subject. 'Will you like being an aide-de-camp?'

'I will let you know that when I have done the job for a bit.'

'You are worried about Christina,' she guessed.

He made a small sound of irritation. 'Not worried, just angry that she still plagues me with her nonsense.'

'What nonsense?'

'Oh, you know the sort of thing . . . references to the past, coy invitations to flattery, a dark hint concerning the most recent of her husband's aides to be killed on the battlefield.'

'She wants you to say how much you admired her when you were together, and reminds you of danger in order to punish you for your rejection of her.'

Alain stared wordlessly at his wife.

Marie-Josèphe just smiled. 'It does not take much in the way of perception to realise that Christina is the kind of woman who never lets go.'

'Do you think I should tell the general that I prefer not to become his aide?'

'Because of a stubborn female? I am surprised at you.'

'As long as you are happy.'

'I am very happy, I thank you, Captain. At this rate you will be a major in no time at all.'

10

Strasbourg
1808

From her vantage point at the drawing-room window on the first floor Christina watched Alain mount the first two steps to the entrance of the Hotel de Montpensier and disappear beneath the portico. The handsome hussar had been her husband's aide for three months and, according to the general, seemed to have settled down well to the rather exacting job; contrary to Emil's flippant predictions it had turned out to be no sinecure.

For the first time in his life Alain had been introduced to paperwork. Lists and requisitions flowed across his desk in an unending stream in the small office which Général Batut had set up in a disused room adjacent to his private apartments. Tables of muskets, carbines and bomb fixtures, requisitions for every piece of military paraphernalia under the sun required his undivided attention, and the days when his time could be idled away between parades and cavalry drill were over. From now on the army must be served by Captain Alain d'Albert in times of truce and in times of war.

Christina continued to watch the traffic, both pedestrian and vehicular, even after the object of her interest had gone beyond her range of vision. Her steady, reflective gaze was fixed upon the ebb and flow taking place in the street below, but she absorbed nothing in detail, for her mind was filled with thoughts of a single human being, one who overshadowed all others in her life. Her outward eye recorded smart carriages and fashionably dressed people, while her inner eye concentrated upon one tall, slim figure.

She had planned for a long time to get Alain back from the woman who had stolen him from her, but fortune had not smiled upon her efforts until she had broken herself of the idiotic habit of clinging to his shadow and had begun to consider possibilities which promised more fruitful returns.

Meeting Lieutenant Latouche had been her first piece of luck. He, unlike Alain, had taken her into Strasbourg society and later had introduced her to his friends as his fiancée, which indeed he thought she was, since he had proposed marriage to her and she had accepted his flattering offer. He had then presented her to his uncle, the general, from whom Christina had evoked an immediate and delighted response. Her animated conversation, which centred almost exclusively upon military matters, both amazed and fascinated the veteran campaigner, and it was not long before he was bluntly suggesting to Christina that she should abandon his nephew in favour of a more mature admirer.

When it became clear to her that

the general was contemplating a rather more loose arrangement than the bonds of matrimony would dictate, Christina had played a daring card and had held out for marriage. Her besotted, ageing lover, a widower of fifty-two, had submitted without a struggle.

Lieutenant Latouche, alternately shattered by the inconstancy of his beloved and consoled by the generosity of his uncle, who bought him off with ten thousand francs, very sportingly retired from the contest. When, several months later and even more sportingly, the general's aide, Lieutenant Garat, dropped dead from a sniper's bullet at Friedland, the way had become clear for Christina to whisper in her doting husband's ear that the newly promoted Captain d'Albert of the 7th Hussars would be the ideal replacement for poor Garat. Captain d'Albert was the one who had gone to see the Emperor about his wounded friend. Had she not heard the general say that he liked the sparky officers, the ones who were not afraid to show a little inventiveness in a crisis?

Having completed her manoeuvres, some of which, as Emil had so shrewdly guessed, had taken place in bed, and seen Alain installed in his new job, Christina had bided her time. Intrigue is both mentally and physically exhausting and she needed a short period in which to recuperate from the frantic machinations of the last few months, a breathing-space which would allow her to prepare herself for the final assault.

Christina turned her eyes away from the window. The final assault would be attempted today.

Alain finished checking the list of replacements to be supplied to the Royal Artillery regiment, which had lost eight howitzers, fifteen mortar ammunition wagons and nine limbers in the Eylau campaign and placed it in a folder for the general's signature. He pulled a silver watch in a shagreen case out of his pocket and studied the dial of the elegant timepiece which had been given to him as a wedding present by Marie-Josèphe. The watch registered half-past two and his stomach was giving out signals indicating its emptiness. He had arranged to meet Emil at the Café Bois-Bleu at half-past three, but the general was out and an extra half hour of idleness might not come amiss after a morning spent poring over his interminable lists. Alain rather hoped the Emperor would go to war again soon. He needed the rest.

He had just picked up his shako when Christina came into the office and shut the door behind her. She was expensively gowned, he noticed, even as he wondered what the hell she wanted. A mocking echo of Emil's voice came to him. 'One of General Victor's aides buys his wife's cap ribbons . . . '

A maxim of the Emperor's, one of many, sprang to his mind. 'If the enemy takes you by surprise, there is no alternative but to go on the defensive.' He turned towards the door. 'Excuse me, Madame, I was just about to go out for dinner.'

She stepped to one side and blocked his way. 'I thought we could have dinner together in my dining-room. I could ask the servants to send in enough for two.'

'Oh, I do not think . . . '

'The general will not be back until late this afternoon.'

'I know, but . . . '

She came a little closer. 'Alain, please. You can have no idea how lonely it is for me imprisoned in this hotel half the day, and how much I envy your wife, who has her child and your mother to keep her company. Surely you would not deny me an hour of pleasant conversation?'

'I have arranged to meet Emil.'

'Oh, Emil.' She laughed. 'He will not pine if you do not turn up. He will engage the attention of the first pretty girl who passes by and ask her to sit down and drink Calvados with him.'

Her accurate assessment of Emil's disposition made him smile, despite his firm determination not to give way to her. The softened look encouraged her.

'Please, Alain. It has been so long since we had a real conversation together. Do you remember how we used to rattle away in that dreadful room in the square and go to the door sometimes to see if Madame La Harpe had her ear pressed to it?'

She looked so elegant and poised and her manner seemed so relaxed — no trace of the old tense and critical Christina could be discerned — that he began to think that it would be churlish of him to refuse her offer of dinner. He reminded himself that she had not gone out of her way to contrive a meeting with him during the months he had worked for her husband. Might he not safely assume that infatuation had died, to be replaced by gentler, less emotional feelings?

He gave a little bow. 'I shall be honoured to accept your kind invitation, Madame.'

Her smile was radiant. 'Splendid! I am so glad that we are friends again, Alain.'

The general's dining-room was comfortable and well-appointed, but Christina had set no mark of her own upon it and remembering her robust attempts at home-making in their dingy lodgings in the cathedral square, Alain wondered why. He came to the conclusion that she did not regard a military headquarters as home, an understandable attitude.

The polished walnut table was big enough to seat twenty people. Christina stationed herself at its head and indicated the chair on her right. 'A dinner party for two,' she smiled.

The covered dishes were brought in, the covers removed and the meal served by quick and experienced hands. When they were alone again Alain said, 'Chicken Marengo, if I am not mistaken. I believe you planned to invite me to dinner today.'

She pleaded guilty. 'I thought it

would be amusing to share a dish of Chicken Marengo with you. Do you remember the last occasion on which we partook of it? You said some rather harsh things to me, I remember, and I fear they were all too true. I am not a good wife.'

'I am sorry if I offended you,' he said uncomfortably.

She waved the apology aside. 'No, no, you were right. Some women are born to be mistresses and others are born to be wives. Against my inclination, I think I must number myself among the former. I shall not be the first person, nor yet the last, to go through life constantly waging war against my natural instincts.'

He sipped at an excellent claret, rolling it round his tongue. 'But you are not unhappy to be the wife of a general?'

She answered surprisingly, 'What is happiness? A state of mind when every day is a joyful experience, or merely a state of bovine contentment? I cannot claim to experience either, but those who have tell me that both can turn one into a social leper, for it is not considered good manners to confess that one has nothing in the world to complain about. Shall I say only that my husband is kind and indulgent towards me when he has the time to spare?'

If she had expected to engage his sympathy she was disappointed. The claret was blotting out sensibility and leaving behind only a masculine sense of superiority over the female sex. He said, 'You should talk to Marie-Josèphe. She is always complaining that I neglect her in favour of a more demanding mistress. She refers, of course, to the army.'

Her eyes shaded at the mention of his wife, but Alain was too busy eating to notice. He had not realised how hungry he was. It was amazing how an excellently prepared meal could set the juices running.

'How is Marie-Josèphe?'

He looked up from his plate to see Christina staring at him in the way that was so familiar, as if she would read his very soul. The steady, concentrated gaze, which revived so many unpleasant memories, disconcerted him and he returned his attention to his plate.

'She is very well, thank you. She is expecting our second child.'

'How splendid. You are becoming quite the family man, Alain.' After a brief pause she went on, 'I wish I could have become friends with Marie-Josèphe. Is it too much to expect that she would welcome any overtures from me?'

His response was brusque. 'Would *you* want to become friends with your husband's former mistress?'

'I do not think I should have any objection to making her acquaintance, provided that she was a woman of taste and refinement. You once told me that your wife was sensible and broad-minded.'

'So she is.'

'But in spite of that she would take exception to a woman who had once had the audacity to sleep in the same bed with her husband?'

The sarcasm was ignored. 'It might be the case. Besides, I imagine you have plenty of friends among the regimental wives.'

'Oh, yes,' she replied carelessly, 'although perhaps it would be more accurate to call them acquaintances. Many of them know all about my past and to them I am the outsider who forced her way into their charmed circle.' Her laugh was brittle. 'Much as they would like to exclude me from that circle, however, they cannot, because I am the general's wife.'

Suddenly he felt rather sorry for her, an entirely new experience for him. Hitherto she had merely angered or irritated him. This claret was quite extraordinarily good.

He said, 'You are right to remind me of my own words. Marie-Josèphe *is* a sensible and broad-minded person.

I shall ask her to call on you.'

She said defensively, 'I should not like her to think that I am desperate for female companionship.'

'Of course not. It may be that she would have called on you before, but hesitated to do so in case of an objection on your part.'

'Or on your part.'

'I shall put no obstacle in the way of your meeting,' he promised.

She seemed pleased. 'Have you finished? I have asked my maid to serve coffee in my private sitting-room. You have time?'

'Another ten minutes will not materially alter the state of army affairs,' he assured her with a smile.

Even Christina's sitting-room had little of her personality stamped upon it. There were no feminine touches, no items of *bric-à-brac*, no artfully arranged flowers. Again this surprised Alain, who recalled the days when she had brightened his lodgings with colourful china jugs purchased at a curio shop and posies of flowers in white china bowls. It did not occur to him that for Christina the two rooms in the square had been home because of his own presence there.

The captain and the general's lady sat down beside each other on a brocaded sofa with a decorous thirty centimetres of space separating them. The coffee tray was brought in by Christina's maid and deposited on a small mahogany table. Christina lifted the slender silver pot, poured streams of steaming brown liquid into delicate china cups and made 'hostess' conversation.

'Will there be another campaign soon, do you think?'

'There is no word of anything yet,' Alain replied, 'but with the Emperor one can never tell. His mind is as busy as the bees embroidered on his robes of state.'

'I wonder if his land-hunger will ever be satisfied? Now that he has decided that England is beyond his grasp, some other country which will not meet his outrageous demands is sure to merit his attention soon, providing him with an excuse to elevate yet another member of his dreadful family to a throne.'

He accepted a cup of coffee. 'I see you still have the same high opinion of the Emperor, who, I feel it my duty to remind you, has done more for France than any other Frenchman since the dawn of time.'

'Italian.'

'What?'

'The Emperor is Italian.'

'By birth only. He took French nationality when he was still a child.' Alain paused reflectively before remarking, 'I am bound to admit that his speech has a decidedly Italian emphasis.'

She smiled. 'Of course. I had forgotten your brave encounter with the conqueror of Europe. By saving Emil's leg Bonaparte has made you his slave for life. Am I not right?'

'You make me sound like a schoolboy with a hero, whereas the truth of the matter is that I have always admired him, as you very well know.'

Alain drained his coffee cup and set it down on the silver tray. 'I must now render thanks for your hospitality, Christina. I have enjoyed your company very much, but it is time I got back to work. I have a list of mortars to draw up which will keep me busy for the entire afternoon.'

He made as if to get up, but she stopped him with a word. 'Alain, I still love you. There will never be anyone else for me. Please do not be angry with me for saying so.'

He told himself that he ought indeed to feel angry with her for leading him along towards this moment, which he now felt sure had been her objective, but he could not. Such persistence as hers surely merited compassion rather than condemnation. For the first time since their relationship had begun Christina, that skilful manipulator of human feelings, had aroused his conscience and he wanted to help her.

But how? How on earth did you make someone fall out of love? Over the years she had argued with him, pleaded with him and caused him endless embarrassment. He had even begun to suspect that her marriage to General Batut had been an act of defiance, aimed directly at him. A declaration of the truth might be a good beginning.

'I love my wife, Christina. You must believe that.'

'I do,' she answered, injecting a convincing note of despair into her voice. 'But cannot you love me too? It is not impossible for a man to love more than one woman at the same time, is it?'

'For me it is impossible.'

She moved nearer to him. 'You were so kind to me once, Alain, so gentle a lover. You were the first man ever to make love to me. I am asking you to make love to me again . . . just once . . . please? If you agree, I swear to you that I will never approach you again.'

She saw by his expression that he found the idea repugnant. 'Why should a single meaningless animal act give you pleasure? What could it mean to either of us?'

She shook her head and covered her face with her hands. 'I just thought . . . '

'A kind of exorcism? Is that what you had in mind?'

'Yes!' She uncovered her face and turned to look at him, her eyes eager and expectant. 'Yes, you have read my thoughts exactly. The laying of a ghost. My father believed in ghosts. He used to claim to see them quite often.'

'I doubt very much whether he ever saw more than a figment of his own imagination.'

Her sigh was nicely calculated to evoke his sympathy. 'Poor father, he always took things so much to heart. I think I have inherited something of his character.'

In what seemed a swift, spontaneous gesture of affection Christina put up her hand to caress Alain's cheek. To his utmost surprise he felt aroused. He had never thought it possible. Memories flooded back of their early days together. Out of the blue — and why should he think of it now? — there rose the image of a summer's evening when he had begun to teach her elementary cavalry tactics and had demonstrated the moves with knives, forks, spoons and a pepper-pot, moving these articles over the surface of an immaculate white tablecloth. He remembered how astonished and delighted he had been at her quick grasp of the subject, the speed with which she had been able to distinguish the respective merits of advancing to the attack *en echiquier* or advancing in echelon. He had felt a certain affection for her then, had he not? There had been something between them, if not love then a strong physical attraction. He felt it now, for the new, more elegantly turned-out, more elegantly-coiffed Christina, who still retained the old, childlike attitude to life and who still failed to understand that it is not always possible to win every game.

He covered the hand on his cheek with his own and gently removed it. Her face fell and her look of disappointment could not quite mask the anger she felt at his continued rejection of her. She had come so close. The scent of victory had been in her nostrils, the taste of it in her mouth before he had snatched it from her in that single, paternal contact, the father removing the sticky hand of his child from his cheek.

She turned her back on him. 'Please go.' Her voice sounded tight, reined in against the rage which threatened to engulf her. Soothing words sprang to his lips, but he did not give them utterance. Something in the way she was sitting, with her body twisted away from him, reminded him of steel about to snap and he obeyed her request without a murmur. Once outside the door he realised that he was shaking.

Christina sat for a long time after

Alain had gone, weeping silently, until all the anger and frustration had drained out of her, to be replaced by the old steely determination to have her own way. The first assault, that is how she had thought of it, and the first assault had so nearly succeeded. The expression on Alain's face when she laid her hand against his cheek had told her everything. He was vulnerable and Marie-Josèphe would soon be growing fat and unwilling as her child blossomed inside her.

Christina wiped away the tears from her face and began to plan her next move.

On the morning after his dangerous encounter with Christina, Alain reported for work and was immediately summoned to the general's study. The brow of his fat, genial superior was furrowed with anxiety. True to his nature he came straight to the point and fired sentences at Alain in approximately five-second bursts.

'My wife has disappeared, Captain.

The servants think she must have slipped out round about six o'clock yesterday evening . . . before I got back. Packed a bag and just went. No sign of a farewell letter. See her yesterday afternoon, did you, while I was out? Seem her usual self to you? Not distressed?'

Alain, suddenly called upon to respond to this fusillade, had little time in which to recover from his astonishment at Christina's disappearance. He struggled to collect his wits and replied as steadily as he could, 'I saw Madame Batut yesterday afternoon, sir, at about half-past two. She was good enough to invite me to have dinner with her. She seemed perfectly composed to me at that time.'

With one stubby forefinger the general stroked the black silk patch which masked his empty eye-socket. The remaining eye was keen and penetrating. 'Had some conversation with her, I suppose? Anything she said strike you as odd?'

'Nothing at all, sir. Madame Batut spoke mainly of the war, and of the possibility of its renewal.'

Before she started trying to seduce me, that is, sir.

Alain almost jumped out of his skin as the general barked at him, 'Know about your affair with my wife, Captain. My nephew told me. Poor boy was jealous and thought it would put me off marrying her. But it made no difference. Old widower like me. Old soldier does not have to think about the social niceties like you younger chaps.'

He paused and began shuffling some papers about on his desk, to no great purpose, Alain observed. The painfully direct eye was fastened once more on his startled subordinate. 'Told you that, Captain, in case you might be holding anything back, something she might have said . . . about me. Thought she was happy . . . might be mistaken.'

'I assure you, sir, there was nothing significant,' Alain said. He said it with firm conviction, knowing that if the poor old fellow suspected for one moment that his wife was in love with another man he would have to call that man out, despite the difference in their respective ranks, and then there would be hell to pay.

To cover the awkward pause which followed Alain asked, 'Do you want me to institute some enquiries, sir, as to Madame Batut's whereabouts? Perhaps she hired a calèche. If I can find the driver of the vehicle, he might remember where he took her.'

The general was shaking his head before Alain had finished speaking. 'I am not one to drag a woman back home by her hair. If she had been abducted that would be a different thing altogether. Wish she had left a note, though. Don't like loose ends.'

'Perhaps Madame Batut's absence will only be temporary, sir,' offered Alain hopefully. 'She may have felt the need to get away from military affairs. The ladies sometimes get very bored with army talk.'

'Not my wife, Captain,' returned the general firmly. 'The Almighty must have had a lapse in concentration when He made her. Forgot to add the parts which would have turned her into a man. She knew more about moving an army from A to B than I know myself. Would have made a damned good quartermaster.'

She learned it all from me, thought Alain, during those evenings we spent together, when she kept hammering away at me with her interminable questions. How does a general get all his troops together in the right place at the right time? How do the men get fed? Where do they sleep on the night before a battle? How does a commander conduct a battle? And he had answered all her questions patiently and meticulously because he was a soldier and soldiering was the one thing he liked to talk about above all else.

The general cut across these reflections. 'Do not misunderstand me,

Captain. I want my wife back, but only if our wishes in that respect coincide. She is the most intelligent and amusing female I have ever come across, when she is not behaving like a child, that is. Curious the way she sometimes gives the impression that her mind has not progressed beyond the age of twelve years. I daresay you noticed that too?'

Alain tried to hide his embarrassment behind some unnecessary throat-clearing. The general seemed to have lost his sense of propriety. To discuss one's wife with her former lover could hardly be considered in the best of taste.

The perpetrator of the *faux pas* appeared to think so too, suddenly becoming conscious of the fact that he had been less than discreet. He mumbled an apology. 'Forgive me, Captain. Mind in a spin. Not thinking what I am saying.'

Alain immediately felt sorry for him. 'Are you quite sure that you do not want me to make some enquiries, sir?

If I can find out where Madame Batut has gone, it may set your mind at rest regarding her welfare?'

The older man shook his head vigorously. 'No, no, leave it. Obliging of you, but leave it. She is young. Probably fed up with an old buffer like me. To tell the truth, Captain, I am too long in the tooth and too set in my ways to stir up a fuss. Got enough on my plate at the moment. The Emperor is talking about invading Spain.'

Alain wondered why Christina's disappearance was causing him so much concern. It was not as if she meant anything to him. He should be raising a cheer to celebrate her desertion of her husband. He had always thought her such a damned nuisance, with her firmly held opinions and her insistence that she could never stop loving him.

An examination of his own feelings forced the conclusion that he was disturbed because the general was disturbed, but the conclusion was not entirely satisfactory. Dammit, he felt guilty about the wretched girl. At this moment he would have given anything to see Christina, to take her in his arms, perhaps, and comfort the poor silly child.

Was it possible that his attitude towards her had changed in as little as twenty-four hours? However much he tried to shy away from the thought by deliberately focussing his mind on his wife and son and the child to come, the answer appeared to be yes. He did not love her, oh no, not that. It was simply that he felt protective towards her. He wanted to try and help her to resolve this anguish of the mind which was causing her to suffer so much.

It was while Alain was wrestling with the ambivalence of his emotions that the idea burst upon his consciousness and he knew, with complete certainty, where Christina had gone.

★ ★ ★

As Alain entered the hallway of the house in the square Madame La Harpe came bustling towards him, looking for all the world as though she had expected him. The spectacles were lowered. 'Good-morning, Monsieur. Your lady is upstairs in the old rooms.'

Your lady. He did not stop to argue, but climbed the stairs two at a time, a little alarmed at his own eagerness, a little surprised by the rapid beating of his heart.

She was sitting by the window looking down into the square and must have seen him enter the house. As he came into the room she turned her head to look at him, presenting him with a grave, unsmiling countenance.

'How did you know that I was here?' Her voice was quiet and controlled.

'I guessed.' He removed his shako and placed it on the table before taking occupancy of one of the shabby old chairs.

'Do you mean to stay here?'

She shook her head. 'I shall return to my husband quite soon, tomorrow perhaps.'

'Then why . . . ?'

'Because I have to get over being alone with you. The experience, contrary to my expectations, has quite unnerved me. Yesterday afternoon, when you had gone, I knew I could not face the prospect of spending the night with Georges. The very thought of it made me feel sick, so I left the hotel and came here. Madame La Harpe was kind to me. She saw that I was unhappy but did not question me as to the reason for my wretched state. I asked her if our old rooms were vacant and when she said they were, I decided to occupy them for a day or two, in order to ponder upon the complexities of my life.'

He could not think of anything to say except, 'The general is very worried about you.'

'Poor Georges. He does not deserve

what I have done to him. Is he looking for me?'

'No, he says he will not force you to return to him, but he would be pleased if you came back because you wanted to.'

'Does he know that you have come here?'

'No.'

She got up from her chair and moved restlessly about the room, clasping and unclasping her hands. 'I am stricken with a deadly disease, Alain, which death alone can cure. I shall love you until I die.'

He made a feeble attempt to jolt her out of her bleak mood. 'How wonderfully consistent you are, my dear.'

'It is the only merit to which I can lay claim.' She stopped her nervous pacing and bent upon him a look both earnest and pleading. 'I think you must care for me a little, Alain, or you would not have bothered to come and find me.'

'I think you are right.'

A smile came and went. 'I should be happy to hear you say that, except that it is not an admission of love.'

'No, rather is it an admission of failure.'

'I do not understand.'

'I should have realised the depth of my own feelings towards you sooner.'

'If you had you would not have married Marie-Josèphe?'

'Ah, now I did not say that. We are all intrinsically selfish, my dear.'

'Selfish enough to sacrifice love for money?'

'Indeed, but I did no such thing. I loved my wife when I married her . . . I love her still . . . I love you . . . there, I have said it.'

'You once told me that it would be impossible for you to love two women at the same time.'

'Ever since I learned to speak I have said a great many unconsidered things.'

She moved to his side and held out her hand which he took in his. 'Are we to become lovers again?'

'It is what people usually do when they are in love.'

A shadow crossed her face. 'Except that this time it will be different. This time we shall be practising a deception because we are no longer free to do as we choose. Shall we meet secretly, once or twice a week, and then return to our respective partners with the lie buried in our hearts?'

He felt her fingers tighten on his hand. 'Oh, Alain, perhaps I should really go away. I am not sure that I could stand the strain of secrecy.'

He pulled her on to his lap. 'You are the most extraordinary woman I have ever known. Even when you thought I was lost to you for ever you refused to accept the inevitable. You refused to let me go. I often wondered what was going through your mind.'

She rested her head against his shoulder. 'When one is crossed in love one fosters all kinds of improbable thoughts.'

The kiss which followed this observation was long and lingering. When they drew apart Alain asked, 'Shall I petition Madame La Harpe on the question of renting these rooms on a month-by-month basis? Because she is a sentimentalist at heart, I think she will agree to let me have them.'

Christina laughed. 'And because she has no morals to speak of.' She kissed his cheek and murmured, 'How wonderful it will be to go back in time. I shall be like the princess in the fairy-tale who has been asleep for a hundred years and wakes to find her prince beside her.'

Alain, having convinced himself that his former pious declaration concerning his capacity for love had been born of ignorance, not to say arrogance, now thought it quite possible that he could share his affections between two women, loving each, if not in the same way, at least with equal fervour. His love for his wife would be a serious and calm affair, that for Christina, a joyous, sensual and amusing experience. He would have the best of both worlds.

As for Christina, while delighted at Alain's capitulation after his protracted and stubborn resistance to every weapon she had been able to produce from her female armoury, it seemed to her that she still had a long way to go before she could consider her triumph complete. It would not please her to share Alain with anyone, least of all with his wife.

11

Strasbourg
1809

In October, 1808, the Emperor sent his troops into Spain in the belief that that country offered easy pickings. The 7th Hussars were not ordered to take part in this venture and Alain spent the whole of that year in Strasbourg. His renewed love affair with Christina added a fresh dimension of excitement to his life and apart from the fact that after more than a year of inactivity he had begun to 'get the itch' for another campaign, he thought himself a very contented man.

He was now the father of two children — Marie-Josèphe had given birth to a daughter in May, 1808, who had been named Helene after her grandmother — and the uncle of one,

Célestine having given birth to a girl at the end of June. He was a well-established family man who harboured a small, insignificant secret which hurt no one. He could even look the general in the eye every morning without the least feeling of unease. Everyone was happy.

In April, 1809, the 7th Hussars were ordered to move across the Rhine. The Emperor had known for some time that there was a spirit of insurrection at large in Austria and another difficult campaign was in prospect.

Two days before the regiment's departure Marie-Josèphe was 'at home' to eight officers' wives; they talked of nothing but the coming campaign. One, the wife of a major, had declared her intention of becoming a 'camp follower', this to the consternation of the other ladies, who professed themselves shocked that she should want to join the ranks of those rather risquée aristocratic women who dogged their campaigning husbands like bloodhounds on the trail of a particularly nasty scent.

'And why should I not?' Madame Dupont had enquired, searching each disapproving face in turn. 'My children are all grown up and I have had enough of being an unofficial widow.'

But the flushed, indignant faces continued to condemn and Madame Dupont felt bound to add, 'General Batut's wife is going with him,' as if this clinched the argument.

There followed an embarrassed silence while everyone tried not to look at Marie-Josèphe. All those present knew that Madame Batut had once been Captain d'Albert's mistress, and it was extremely tactless of Madame Dupont to mention her name in this house of all places.

Marie-Josèphe, seemingly unaware of the flutters of distress among her doves, concentrated only on the performance of her duties as a hostess and kept a watchful eye on empty plates and cups. The awkward moment passed.

When the ladies had taken their leave, however, she felt a headache threatening and decided to walk in the garden, where the swaying heads of daffodils and narcissi heralded the approach of summer.

The young woman was grateful that her children were out with their nursemaid and that her mother-in-law had retired for her afternoon rest. She had the garden to herself. The swing which Alain had constructed for the enjoyment of his adventurous son caught her eye and she went to sit on it, propelling herself gently to and fro. The motion of the swing relaxed her and some of the tensions of the day drained away, but the headache persisted.

Madame Dupont's thoughtless remark had brought back memories, but not in the way the other ladies might have thought. They knew only that Christina had been a part of Marie-Josèphe's past, not that she had unexpectedly come leaping into the present. Just two days ago Christina had blasted Marie-Josèphe's world into smithereens when she had walked out of a house in the cathedral square on the arm of Captain Alain d'Albert. Marie-Josèphe was not in the habit of visiting the square in the old part of the town, a fact of which her husband was aware, and which doubtless had caused him to be careless; but there is always a first time for everything and the first time had come for Marie-Josèphe after one of her friends told her that an ex-patriate Englishman had opened up a hat boutique in that vicinity. Alain did not know about the hat boutique, or of his wife's interest in it. Alain did not expect Marie-Josèphe to go to the square.

At first Marie-Josèphe had not believed the evidence of her own eyes. She saw but she did not see, and when at last the realisation dawned that it was indeed Alain, her husband, whom she had seen looking down into Christina's laughing, upturned face, the two figures upon which every faculty she possessed had been concentrated, had disappeared.

She walked home with her mind in turmoil and without the least idea what, if anything, she meant to do about her discovery. A return of calmness brought with it a more rational analysis of her situation. She felt both anger and despair at her husband's betrayal of her, with despair uppermost. He did marry me for my money after all, she thought, and his much-vaunted detestation of Christina was proclaimed in order to deceive me. Second thoughts discounted this conclusion. She was certain that Alain had been in love with her when he married her, and that he loved her still. It was just that Christina could give him something which it was not in her power to give him, something which an inhibiting delicacy forbade her to give him. The thought made her blush.

The question Marie-Josèphe asked herself now as she swung backwards and forwards was, Shall I confront Alain with my knowledge of his unfaithfulness, or is it better to say and do nothing? It was difficult to come to a decision over this important matter with her head pounding away. But ideas can come into flower, despite painful distractions, and one bloomed for Marie-Josèphe now. Like Madame Dupont she would become a 'camp follower', not merely to be with Alain on campaign during the intervals between the fighting, but to carry out a rather more positive design.

Marie-Josèphe parted from her husband with the customary endearments and the customary affectionate admonishments concerning his well-being. Also in accordance with custom he laughed at her ritually expressed fears and promised not to sleep in a wet uniform or waterlogged boots. They both knew the promise would be broken many times, but the knowledge was never allowed to surface. The wet uniform conversation, repeated so often, was like a talisman which they both cherished, a hostage to fortune and an earnest of the soldier's safe return.

When Alain had gone, leaving the imprint of his kisses lingering on her mouth, Marie-Josèphe broke the news of her bold intention to her mother-in-law. As she had anticipated, the Countess strongly disapproved of it.

'Women who follow their husbands to war,' she declared, with severe emphasis on every word, 'do it not for the sake of their husbands, but for their own personal gratification. They foresee infinite possibilities of delight in being entertained at soirées and balls, and when their men march out to fight they stay behind in the place where the Emperor has set up his headquarters, and continue going to soirées and balls as though their very lives depended upon it. I wonder whether the selfish creatures ever spare a thought for the hardships which the soldiers are forced to endure. In my opinion they are no better than the loose women who march with the common soldiers ... No, indeed, they are a great deal worse, for the prostitutes share the hardships of their men and tend them when they are wounded.'

Marie-Josèphe said not a word during this tirade, nor did she speak when the Countess paused to draw breath. The older woman eyed her curiously. 'I find it quite remarkable that Alain made no mention of your joining him at Stuttgart before he went off. Am I to assume that he knows nothing of your rash intention?'

Marie-Josèphe rejoined quietly, 'Alain does not know what I mean to do.'

'If he had known he would have forbidden you to do it.'

'Yes.'

'And what of your son? What am I to tell him when his mother disappears from his sight? He is of an age to pine for you.'

'You know he adores you, *Maman.* You will spoil him so much that he will be quite sorry to see me on my return. And I know that Célestine will help. If I ask her, she will bring little Adèle to play with Claude, and she will take all the children out for walks in the park.'

The austere features of the Countess expressed surprise. 'Oh, so I am to be faced with a conspiracy? Célestine is to be made your ally in this. I find it interesting that you should be so sure of my daughter's co-operation.'

The two women were still standing in the entrance hall of the house, where they had so recently made their farewells to Alain. Marie-Josèphe laid her hand on the arm of her mother-in-law.

'Please, *Maman*, do not be cross. I see now that there is something I must tell you. Shall we go into the drawing-room?'

The Countess inclined her head, her face softening into a smile. 'I knew you were not like those others, my dear, to whom I made reference in such derogatory terms, and I apologise for condemning you unheard. However, I feel obliged to remind you that you are as precious to me as Célestine and to say that it grieves me terribly to think that you would hesitate in the least degree before confiding in me.'

Marie-Josèphe accepted the rebuke meekly, murmured, 'I am sorry,' and followed the Countess into the drawing-room.

When both women were seated the younger remained silent for several minutes. Wisely, the other did not prompt her to begin her explanation, but set herself calmly to work on a piece of embroidery which lay on the table beside her chair.

'I think, no, I *know*, that Alain and Madame Batut have become lovers . . . again.'

The Countess was so startled, as much by the suddenness of Marie-Josèphe's announcement as by its unexpected content, that she pricked her finger. She recovered her composure quickly to ask, 'What makes you think that such is the case?'

Marie-Josèphe's eyes filled with tears as she answered miserably, 'Because I saw them come out of that house in the cathedral square where Alain used to live before his marriage to me. No. 42 was it?' — and as the Countess gave a reluctant but confirming nod — 'They were walking arm in arm and they were looking at each other in that special way . . . you know?'

The Countess gave no indication as to whether she knew about 'special looks' or not, but after a pause she said, 'You appear to think that by going to Stuttgart you can do something to alter the situation, but I ask you this, my dear, is it wise to tell Alain that you suspect he has taken that woman for his mistress when he is about to go into battle? If there is one thing I have learned from having a soldier son it is that the distraction of unhappy thoughts when a man is about to engage the enemy can result in a swift and bloody end.'

'I am not going to Stuttgart to see Alain,' replied Marie-Josèphe, absent-mindedly pleating the skirt of her silk dress into tiny folds, 'I am going to see *her*. I shall put up at some small hotel just outside the city and when the army moves out I shall go to the Hotel Augustus in the Marienstrasse — that is where the 7th Hussars are to establish their temporary headquarters — and I shall ask for Madame Batut. If she will consent to see me I shall tell her that she is to keep away from my husband.'

The Countess regarded her daughter-in-law with sad eyes. 'How very angry you are. And you think that by confronting this woman and telling her that you know of her liaison with Alain it will make any difference?'

'I do not think she is a truly bad woman. If I tell her how unhappy I am she may agree to end the affair.'

'And what if she does? Do you think

that Alain will agree to end the affair too? Or do you think perhaps that he might be very angry indeed that you have interfered in his life?'

Marie-Josèphe started up and with heightened colour protested, 'His life *is* my life. How can I be accused of interfering in something which belongs to both of us?'

'Is it so awful that Alain should want to keep a small part of his life separate from yours?'

'Yes,' came the immediate response. 'To me it is dreadful to be betrayed by my own husband.'

The Countess smiled slightly. 'Betrayal is such an emotive word. I never regarded my own husband's infidelity in that light.'

Marie-Josèphe could not conceal her astonishment at this sudden revelation. 'Oh, I am sorry,' was all she could think of to say.

'Do not be sorry, my dear,' returned the Countess. 'It was all such a long time ago. I mention it now only because my own reactions to such a situation, similar to that in which you now find yourself, may be of some help to you in resolving it.

'Before I say any more, however, I must tell you that I loved my husband very dearly and he, I know, loved me. On the day those creatures who called themselves the leaders of the French government murdered him, I wanted to die too and indeed, had it not been for Alain and Célestine, I would have found a way to contrive my own doom, even though it would have meant the damnation of my soul. But the one thing Claude would never have forgiven me for was the desertion of our children, and it was that certain knowledge that stayed my hand.'

As she opened her heart to her daughter-in-law, the Countess continued to work steadily, pushing a shining thread of blue silk in and out of a linen tablecloth. She brought her story to an end with these words: 'As to the woman who became his mistress, I never set eyes on her, although I knew who she was. She was an actress from the *Comédie Française*, a pretty thing by all accounts. Men are so strange. Claude never knew that I was aware of his association with her, and I never told him I knew. It would have served no purpose, except to burden him with guilt. We loved each other, you see, just as you and Alain love each other.'

The beautiful Meissen porcelain clock on the chimney-piece ticked away sixty seconds of silence before Marie-Josèphe said quietly, 'It is not in my nature to play the submissive wife. Alain is doing something which hurts me deeply and I must try to make him stop it.'

'You will succeed only in angering him,' came the cold rejoinder.

'Then justice will have been done, for he has angered me. You were born into the aristocracy, *Maman*, a closed society where people are taught from a very early age to hide their feelings, because it is considered unmannerly to put them on public show. I, on the other hand, am the daughter of a humble tradesman. I hope you will not be offended when I say that I think it is better in marriage to be frank and open and that I do not believe that you were not hurt by your husband's infidelity.'

'I was hurt, yes,' responded the Countess, 'but I think I should have been hurt even more if I had tried to wean my husband away from his mistress. As to the aristocracy not showing their feelings, it may surprise you to learn that my dearest friend killed her husband's mistress before turning the knife upon herself and chose, moreover, a most public place in which to perform her ghastly deeds. It is not training which counts in matters of the heart, it is temperament.'

'I am determined to go to Stuttgart,' Marie-Josèphe insisted stubbornly.

The Countess gave in with a sigh. 'I am not surprised. I had hoped to turn you from your purpose, but with no very great expectation of doing so. All I ask is that you will come back home as soon as you have made your attempt, for I shall be very lonely without you.'

Marie-Josèphe rose and bending over her mother-in-law, kissed her cheek. 'I shall come back very soon, *Maman*,' she promised.

12

Marie-Josèphe had not told her mother-in-law the whole truth about her reasons for wanting to confront Christina. It would have been impossible to do so, for those reasons were bizarre in the extreme. She even thought so herself, but there was a certain fitness to her plan, even a certain élan which appealed to the dormant skittishness in her personality.

She made the journey to Stuttgart in her own coach, accompanied only by her personal maid, Elisabeth, who was under the impression that her mistress had succumbed to the lure of pre-battle balls and theatre parties. That such was not the case became apparent when Madame d'Albert put up at a small

271

hotel on the outskirts of the bustling city and informed the proprietor of the modest establishment that she would only be staying for a few days.

Elisabeth was puzzled by the shortness of the proposed stay, but it was not her place to ask questions. There were plenty she would have liked to ask. To take two examples: Why had not Madame d'Albert gone into Stuttgart and made enquiries for her husband? Could it possibly be that she was meeting a lover? Elisabeth hoped not; a simple, country-bred girl, she believed in the sanctity of the marriage vows.

Elisabeth had barely had time to unpack Marie-Josèphe's single small trunk, however, when she was faced with a request from its owner which seemed to confirm her worst fears. It was that she would go into Stuttgart and find out when the regiments were to move out. Her meek 'Certainly, Madame,' followed by a look of deep reproach, brought laughter.

'Pray, do not look at me like that,

Elisabeth,' Marie-Josèphe admonished her. 'I am not about to make an assignation with a lover, you foolish girl, nor is it any business of yours if I were. Now go and fetch your basket, for there are one or two purchases I wish you to make for me when you go into the city.'

Elisabeth's mission proved simpler than she had anticipated. While walking down the Königstrasse she had been accosted by a cheerful corporal with a request for 'a half-hour of your company, sweetheart,' an invitation which she had indignantly rejected. The corporal had merely shrugged and apologised quite politely. 'I am sorry, Mademoiselle, that I took you for a dishonest woman, but our regiment has orders to move out tomorrow morning and who knows if we shall be back, or lying on some field as food for the crows?'

The remark had been delivered with the clear intention of eliciting sympathy from the pretty young woman, but it failed lamentably of its purpose. Elisabeth, for all her youth, was wise in the ways of common soldiers. 'When they taste you, the crows will spit you out, soldier,' she retorted spiritedly, and with a most flirtatious flick of her skirt disappeared into a baker's shop.

Marie-Josèphe was very much relieved when she learned that the regiments were to move out so soon. The feeling that she might weaken in her resolve to see Christina if the waiting proved too long was growing stronger by the hour. She knew she must act quickly before the headquarters staff packed up and moved on down the line of march.

The afternoon of the following day saw Marie-Josèphe entering her coach, minus the perplexed Elisabeth, and instructing her man to drive her to the Hotel Augustus. Having sent up her card she then waited, confident in the expectation that Christina's curiosity would overcome any reluctance she might feel at the prospect of meeting her lover's wife. Five minutes later that confidence was justified. A servant brought down a message which stated that Madame Batut would be pleased to receive Madame d'Albert.

Marie-Josèphe alighted from her coach, gave instructions for the vehicle to be at her disposal in one hour's time, and entered the Hotel Augustus, ignoring the butterflies in her stomach which did their best to deter her from her purpose.

Christina received her unexpected guest with a pleasant but cautious smile and invited her to sit down, pointing to an overstuffed chair upholstered in blue velveteen. 'I hate hotel rooms,' she said. 'The furniture and pictures are never to one's taste.'

It was a remark designed to put herself at ease rather than to assure Marie-Josèphe of her desire to be friendly. The latter, appearing perfectly composed, settled herself into the chair and fixed her adversary — for as such she regarded her — with the steady look of a duellist sizing up his opponent. She might have been staring down the barrel of a pistol. Christina felt distinctly uncomfortable, even a little resentful to be the target of that autocratic stare. Why had Alain's wife come to see her? What did she want from her? Had she stumbled upon the truth?

Marie-Josèphe broke the strained silence. 'Do you mean to stay here in Stuttgart for the duration of the campaign, Madame, or is it your intention to follow the line of march?'

'I was going to ask the very same thing of you, Madame d'Albert,' countered Christina. 'I had not heard that you were to come here.'

'Why should you have heard? Perhaps you are under the mistaken impression that Alain knew I was coming, and knowing, would naturally have notified *you* of the fact?'

A small sigh escaped Christina, but she made no attempt to counterfeit surprise or shock. She said simply, 'So you know about Alain and me?'

'I found out that you were seeing each other quite by chance. You must not blame Alain for being indiscreet.'

It seemed to Christina that Marie-Josèphe was waiting for her to make some comment upon the tangled situation. A light shrug indicated her helplessness. 'So, you have come here, I suppose, to vent your anger upon me, or perhaps to ask me to end my relationship with Alain?'

'No,' the other replied off-handedly, 'I have come to do neither of those things.'

'Then what is your purpose in seeking this meeting?' Christina sounded impatient.

'I have come to challenge you to a duel.'

The younger woman's eyes opened wide. 'Alain always said you had a sense of humour.'

'I think I have, but at this moment I am in deadly earnest. I am even a little angry now that I have discovered that my personal characteristics have come under discussion between my husband and his *friend*.'

Christina leant back in her chair with her rival's level gaze resting upon her. She looked as though someone had punched her in the stomach and knocked the breath out of her.

'I am in earnest,' repeated Marie-Josèphe slowly.

'I believe you are.'

'Alain told me that he taught you to fence.'

'Yes, he did.'

'He taught me too. I thought it would be interesting to find out which one of us had proved to be the most promising pupil. Forgive me, but you are looking at me as if you think I am mad.'

'Jealousy, they say, is first cousin to insanity.'

'Jealousy? Yes, it is a horrid word and a horrid emotion to experience, so humiliating, so destructive to the spirit. That is why I must resolve the matter of Alain's betrayal of me, one way or the other.'

'How, resolve it?'

'We fight for him.'

Christina smiled slightly. 'And whoever is the victor may claim Alain as her prize?'

'I am sure you realise that it is not quite as simple as that. I am the mother of Alain's children. If I should win I shall expect you to give him up for ever. On the other hand, if I should lose, *you* are not to expect that I shall go out of his life altogether. I shall still be his wife, but I shall make no attempt to stop him from seeing you.'

'And if I do not agree?'

'Then I shall take my children and I shall go away somewhere. Alain will never see me, or them, again.'

'I might be very happy for you to do that. Why should I fight you when I can have what I want simply by refusing to take part in your absurd charade?'

'Because the present arrangement

must suit you very well. You have a complacent husband and a contented lover, but if your lover loses his wife and children he may not be so contented. He may become morose and disagreeable and blame you for being the cause of his wretched condition. Eventually, he will almost certainly abandon you.'

Marie-Josèphe fingered the gold wedding-band on her finger, a gesture both unconscious and symbolic, and finished almost pleadingly, 'I shall be fighting for my happiness, Christina. Will not you fight for yours?'

It is not uncommon for the enunciation of a single word to trigger off a mechanism in the human brain which releases a whole new set of contradictory emotions, and so it was now. The intimate use of her Christian name completely changed the emphasis of this extraordinary conversation for Christina. She was no longer playing hostess to her lover's wife, the distant, unapproachable Madame d'Albert, possessed of a vast fortune and with powerful connections. The woman sitting opposite to her, dressed in an immaculate gown of lemon-coloured silk and with a straw, silk-edged bonnet decorated with ribbons and flowers on her head, was her fellow-contender in the lists of love . . . and her equal in society. Marie-Josèphe had judged her opponent and her moment well.

'The rules of this contest,' Christina said, still with that slight, uncertain smile hovering about her lips. 'You have already indicated that we are not to fight to the death. Therefore, who is to judge where the victory lies?'

'The first to draw blood will be declared the winner,' replied Marie-Josèphe.

'But the drawing of blood may testify to a fatal wound,' protested her astonished listener.

Marie-Josèphe brushed this consideration aside. 'Ours will be a contest of skill only. High emotions will not come into it. You will agree with me that it is necessary for one's feelings to be heavily engaged to produce a fatal outcome?'

'In theory, yes, but there is always the possibility of a mistake, an error of judgement.'

'But I shall not go into the contest imbued with the desire to kill you. Nor, I think, will it be your desire to kill me.'

There was something a little chilling in the way Marie-Josèphe gave utterance to this last remark, but Christina had allowed herself to be drawn too far. To retreat now would be tantamount to an admission of faint-heartedness. She said, 'I think you must have already determined where our trial of arms is to take place?'

'This city is surrounded by woods,' came the immediate reply. 'There is a very secluded spot, just beyond the village of Ausberg. I marked it on my way here. I suggest that we ride out to the place early tomorrow morning. We can hire horses from this hotel.'

'Are there to be any witnesses to our contest?'

'Only our maids, and they will be led to believe that we are indulging in an eccentric exercise for our own amusement.'

'Eccentric to a degree,' rejoined Christina. 'And what are we to wear for the performance? It seems to me that fashionable gowns cannot be regarded as practical duelling garb.'

'You have a riding habit?'

'Of course.'

'Then wear that. One hand to hold a sword and the other to hold up one's skirt is all that is required.'

'Swords, yes, we shall require swords. I would be willing to wager that you have in your possession at this very moment two suitable weapons.'

'They belong to Alain.'

'Naturally.' Christina's smile seemed fixed into place by some mechanical means. 'It would be indelicate of us to fight with anything else.'

'We shall not be like the men

and observe all the foolish rituals of duelling,' Marie-Josèphe said. 'We shall simply salute each other and begin.'

'We shall salute each other and begin. How charming!'

'I judge that you are willing to accept my challenge?'

'My dear Marie Josèphe, how could I refuse such an unexceptionable offer?'

'Good, then I shall meet you here at six o'clock tomorrow morning and we will ride in the direction of Ausberg together, with our maids taking the pillions. I think that is the best arrangement. If we were to proceed separately and alone to the rendezvous, we might become objects of unwelcome curiosity to passers-by.'

'And how shall we carry our swords? Hidden under our cloaks, or disguised as parasols?'

The humour of the remark seemed to elude Marie-Josèphe, who answered seriously, 'I shall wrap them in a cloth and carry them across my saddle-bow.'

It was at this point in the extraordinary

conversation that Christina fell prey to creeping doubts. Alain had already accused her of making him the laughing-stock of the regiment. How would he react if it ever came to his knowledge that his wife and his mistress had fought a duel over him? Secrets, however carefully preserved, are all too often revealed by some totally unforeseen circumstance over which those party to them have no control.

Doubts breed fears and Christina said anxiously, 'I would prefer it if you were not to bring your maid to our rendezvous. The girl has been in your service for a long time and may know something of the history of our connection.'

'You are having second thoughts,' Marie-Josèphe accused.

'There you are wrong, but surely it has occurred to you that if Alain finds out through your maid that we have been fighting a duel — and it is not beyond the bounds of possibility that she may stumble upon the truth — we may both lose him.'

'For my part, I am prepared to take that chance, because I know that Elisabeth is completely loyal to me,' answered Marie-Josèphe. 'However, if her presence will cause you anxiety, I shall leave her behind, on condition that you will agree to bring your maid. We must have someone to hold our hats and cloaks and look after the horses.'

Christina gave a reluctant nod. 'My girl does not know you. She has been in my service for only three weeks.'

'Then that is settled. I hope you are entirely satisfied now with our arrangements?'

'As satisfied as anyone can be who is about to make a fool of herself.'

'Oh, come, do not say that. I am told that in Paris it is all the rage for fashionable ladies to challenge each other to mock-duels, from which they derive a great deal of harmless amusement. In more serious vein, I would remind you that I do mean to stand firm by my resolve to leave Alain if you should decide to back out of our arrangement at the last minute. Be sure that he will blame you for my desertion of him. Men are so irrational when it comes to an examination of their own feelings, so prone to think that, as the superior species, they must be in the right. Do you not agree?'

'I agree that you leave me no choice.'

Marie-Josèphe smiled. 'That was my intention . . . to leave you no choice.'

★ ★ ★

The morning dawned with a blushing pink sky which slowly gave way to a clear, translucent blue. Flocks of chaffinches swept low over the house-tops and a clutch of thrushes perched with military precision along the ridge tiles of the Hotel Augustus, in anticipation of discarded scraps of bread and meat which sometimes turned up in the kitchen courtyard.

Early risers took little notice of three

women, one riding pillion, who trotted towards the town gate on indifferent hired hacks. The good citizens of Stuttgart had their own business to attend to. The hordes of the Emperor of France had departed and it was going to be a lovely spring day.

It took the travellers an hour to reach their destination, at first following the main road and then branching off on to a winding, steeply inclined woodland path which terminated in a small clearing carpeted with beech-mast and last year's fallen and decaying leaves. It was a glade such as children love to play in, a make-believe kingdom inhabited by tiny red and grey squirrels which popped out from behind trees in startled recognition of the invaders, and darted away again to hide until the danger was past.

After the three had dismounted and tethered the horses, Christina, who was wearing a dark blue riding habit cut with masculine severity, took her maid to one side and addressed her thus:

'Madame d'Albert and I, Julie, have come here this morning to practise our swordsmanship. It is quite the fashion nowadays for ladies to cross swords, so pray do not be alarmed. There will be no malice in our contest.'

Julie's face, far from showing alarm, displayed tremendous enthusiasm. 'Oh, Madame, how exciting! My young man is a trumpeter in the de Berchèny regiment and I have often watched him practising sword-play with his friends. I know all the movements.'

Christina, meeting the eager brown eyes and observing the healthily glowing cheeks of her maid, was tempted to smile. 'Then you shall be our judge, and we shall leave it to you to decide which of us is the better performer.'

Both ladies now removed their cloaks and hats and gave them to Julie, who folded the former neatly and placed them, topped by the hats — one blue, one crimson — side by side on a fallen tree-trunk, the other end of which was to serve as her viewing-stand for the exhibition.

Marie-Josèphe unwrapped the swords and offered her opponent first choice. Christina took the one nearest to hand, saying, 'I think there can be little advantage to be gained from making a choice?'

'None at all,' replied her opponent. 'They are weapons of an identical weight and design.'

'I trust neither is too sharp?'

'Not too sharp,' the other confirmed. 'You need have no fear. Now back away from me until we are two sword-lengths apart.'

This manoeuvre having been completed, Marie-Josèphe gathered up the skirt of her habit in her left hand and kicked away a loose stone. 'Julie, come here!' she called.

The girl obeyed, running across to where the two women stood facing each other. 'Take off your kerchief,' commanded Marie-Josèphe, 'and hold it above your head. When you bring it down we shall begin.'

'Just like a real duel,' Julie giggled and removing her kerchief from her head, carried out her order. 'Are you ready, my ladies?'

Both signified assent with a nod and the kerchief came down with a sharp snap.

With prudent haste Julie retired to her makeshift seat and watched the initial circling movements of the ladies with a critical eye. Her first thought was that Madame d'Albert seemed lighter on her feet than the younger Madame Batut. All the same, it was Marie-Josèphe who made the first move, with a forward thrust of her sword aimed at the other's stomach.

Christina leapt back, almost letting go of her skirt and exclaimed indignantly, 'Take care! You almost hit me.'

'I was nowhere near you,' laughed Marie-Josèphe, 'and anyway, you should not lower your guard like that. I thought you said that Alain taught you to fight like a cavalryman.'

Christina began to feel an uneasiness not far removed from fear. Had she underestimated Marie-Josèphe, casting her in the role of contented wife and mother and ignoring what might lie hidden beneath that calm exterior? Was there a tigress concealed by the elegant riding habit of crimson velvet, waiting to leap out at her, crouching for the kill . . . a tigress with a teasing smile, who was already looking for another opening?

Her opponent's sword flickered before her eyes like the tongue of a snake and uneasiness was replaced by full-blown fear, allied to a burning anger which released a flow of adrenalin into her veins and quickened the pace of the fight.

Julie, perched on her tree-trunk, became transfixed by the spectacle being enacted before her eyes. The ladies were almost as good as the men, so good that the casual observer might be forgiven for mistaking play for the real thing. Both wore expressions of intense concentration.

The watching girl gave a little gasp as simultaneous thrusts brought the two so close together that they locked arms. With eyes staring and teeth clenched they strained against each other and broke away at last, only to begin the fight all over again. Julie could hear the harsh intakes and exhalations of breath. She began to wish they would stop, but consoled herself with the thought that the swords would most certainly have been blunted before the ladies began to play such a dangerous game.

Almost before this idea had unravelled itself in Julie's head, however, Marie-Josèphe's sword chopped downwards, leaving behind it a long cut on Christina's left cheek. The latter dropped her sword and fell to her knees, even as Julie's scream filled the spring morning and a rustle of small woodland animals responded with agitated scamperings.

Marie-Josèphe stood as if turned to stone, gaping at her bloody handiwork. With her hand pressed to her wounded face Christina stared up at her angrily. 'You bitch! It was your intention to mark my face if you could . . . to make me ugly for him!'

An anguished cry was torn from Marie-Josèphe and tears filled her eyes. 'No! No! I never wanted to hurt you, I swear it. Before God, I swear it.'

'You wanted to kill me. I saw it in your face.'

'No!'

A little way off Julie was sobbing with her face buried in her hands. Christina yelled at her, 'Be quiet, you stupid girl and bring me your kerchief before I bleed to death. For God's sake, hurry!'

Julie, aroused by the familiar tone of command, sprang to her feet and came running towards her mistress with the kerchief held out stiffly in front of her, as if she were anxious for the piece of lawn to reach its destination in the shortest possible time.

Christina, struggling to stand up, almost snatched it from her and applied it to her streaming face. Oblivious now of Julie's listening presence, she demanded of Marie-Josèphe, 'So now are you satisfied? You have drawn first blood and the victory is yours.'

All the colour had drained from Marie-Josèphe's face. She too seemed to have forgotten the presence of a third party and said, low-voiced, 'I cannot share him with you. I would rather die.'

'What if I were to tell you the same thing, that I would rather die than share him with *you*?'

'I should not believe you. You simply want that which you cannot have.'

'How little you know me. I love Alain with all my heart.'

'But you will keep to your side of our bargain?'

Christina suddenly became aware of Julie's wide brown eyes resting disapprovingly upon her and ordered her sharply to retrieve the hats and cloaks. Her eyes returned to the silent and subdued woman standing before her. 'A strange bargain indeed, when we are both prepared to risk disfigurement for the love of a man. It occurs to me that at this very moment Alain may be going to his death and that this comedy of ours will be all for nothing. I cannot make up my mind which of us is the bigger fool, you for initiating the enterprise, or I for agreeing to take part in it. However, if it will please you to hear me say it, I give you my word that from henceforth Alain and I will cease to be lovers.'

The journey back to Stuttgart was conducted in total silence. When Marie-Josèphe insisted on accompanying Christina to her hotel the other, who was still holding the blood-soaked kerchief to her face, made no objection. Nor did she object when, upon arrival at the hotel, it was suggested that a doctor should be sent for. Back in her room she sat, silent and motionless, while Julie brought her cushions and Marie-Josèphe sent down an order for lemon tea.

When the doctor, a thin, serious young man, arrived, he was informed, rather sheepishly, by Marie-Josèphe that she and Madame Batut had been practising their skills with swords when the unfortunate accident had occurred. The doctor, who was quite used to the eccentricities of ladies of fashion, was nonetheless both shocked and disapproving, and after examining Christina's cheek pronounced judgement in solemn tones: 'You will have a scar on your face for the rest of your life, Madame. The cut is quite deep, but it will heal more quickly if it is exposed to the air. I will give you some ointment to apply to the wound which will soothe the soreness.'

The young man's look of reproach deepened as he opened his bag and began sorting through its contents. 'I hope you will not be offended if I suggest that sword-play is hardly a suitable pastime for ladies. Pray consider how your face will disgust the onlooker in the years to come. You will no doubt wish to wear a veil until the mark is less noticeable. Now, if you will permit, I will first apply this tincture of iodine to clean the wound. It is the latest medical discovery and is proving wonderfully efficient at preventing infections.'

While he worked the patient said nothing, nor, the doctor observed, did her anxious friend. After the completion of his ministrations he departed with the briefest of salutations.

Christina came out of her trance-like state to remark cuttingly, 'So, the sight of my face will disgust the onlooker according to the good doctor. What a delightful prospect!' She rounded on Marie-Josèphe, one forefinger indicating the inflamed gash on her cheek which the doctor had treated with an evil-looking green ointment over the yellow stain of the iodine. 'My duelling scar. Do you approve of it? Shall I wear it with pride?'

'Stop! Oh, please, stop!' Marie-Josèphe got up from her chair and went to stand by the window, looking down almost with longing at the street below, where untroubled people were going about their business. She felt stifled in the large ugly room, and yearned to be back in Strasbourg with her mother-in-law and her children, yearned to occupy herself with the repetitive tasks of everyday living. What devil was it which had taken possession of her mind and prompted her to do things so alien to her nature?

'Perhaps I should join the army,' Christina was saying in that harsh, unnatural voice. 'I should make a handsome hussar. Do you not think so? In the army my scar would merit much flattering attention and in no time at all I should become the toast of the ladies, who would fall over themselves in their efforts to attract my attention.'

A tap at the door announced the arrival of the lemon tea. Julie took the tray from the hotel servant and looked enquiringly at her mistress. 'Shall I pour the tea, Madame?'

'Call me sir,' came the loud response. 'From now on, Julie, I am your master, the gallant Captain Batut.'

Julie pressed her lips tightly together and carefully dispensed the tea into small china cups. After handing the cups to the ladies she departed without a backward glance at the disgraceful pair of brawlers.

Christina, in her new rôle, was both embarrassing and unstoppable. 'Do come and sit down,' she said to her uncomfortable guest. 'You look quite ridiculous standing there with a cup and saucer balanced on the palm of your hand.'

Marie-Josèphe complied reluctantly with this request, feeling as though she were humouring a child. Christina smiled at her brightly and the other had to force herself not to turn her eyes away from the ghastly, sticky mess for which she herself must take the responsibility, a combination of congealed blood, iodine and paste which made her feel sick.

Christina was all too well aware of the effect she was having on Alain's wife and thought herself entitled to this minor triumph. She held her adversary in the grip of a firm and challenging stare. 'Tell me, what do you think of my idea? Do you think I shall make a good soldier, a loyal servant of the Emperor, who is the saviour of France?'

Marie-Josèphe, perceiving that Christina's odd mood was undoubtedly occasioned by shock, treated the question seriously. 'You might make a very good soldier. As to being loyal to the Emperor, I gather from your tone that you have no very high opinion of him.'

'He is such an arrogant man.'

'How on earth do you know that?'

'A man's character is represented in his actions.'

'Which so far have been of great benefit to France. There are many who really do think of him as the saviour of our nation.'

'Oh, I am quite sure that he thinks of himself as God, and in the present climate of atheism the people probably think he is too.'

'My husband admires him.'

Christina's lip curled. 'Your husband does not believe he is divine. He admires him because he is a good general.'

Marie-Josèphe's patience snapped. 'There is no need to remind me that we both know a great deal about Alain.'

Christina's eyes were bright with anger. 'I came into his life before you.'

'And should have gone out of it when he married me.' Marie-Josèphe put down her cup and stood up. 'If only you had not persisted in your obsessive attachment to him.'

'My obsessive attachment? Do you think you are the only woman in the world capable of truly loving Alain? I love him and why should my love be any less sincere than yours?'

'Please, let us not continue this conversation,' Marie-Josèphe said. 'It can give neither of us any satisfaction. I understand your anger and can only repeat that I did not mean to hurt you. I trust that for your part you will adhere to your promise not to persist in your attachment to Alain. If it is of any interest to you, I shall return to Strasbourg tomorrow and there is a place in my carriage for you should you require it. I think you can have nothing more to do here.'

When Marie-Josèphe had gone, Christina sat for some time with her head in her hands. Alain would never know now that she was carrying his child. While she had fought with Marie-Josèphe she had thought of the child and had been alarmed for its safety, bitterly reproaching herself for her weakness in allowing herself to be drawn into the bizarre contest. But by then it had been too late. She had come up against a woman as determined as herself not to lose the man she loved, a woman who outclassed her in ingenuity and primitive female savagery, the sweet and loving Marie-Josèphe. There was really only one thing left for her to do.

13

Wagram
July, 1809

Alain and Emil stood with their backs to a tree, allowing the sturdy trunk of the beech to act as a prop for their exhausted frames. Both were a mass of cuts and bruises, but neither had sustained a serious injury. What was left of their once smart uniforms hung upon them in tattered lengths of cloth, making a mockery of buttons, cords and gold epaulettes, those cheerful adornments to the battle-dress of a hussar. Emil's sabre was broken and his mount lay dead on the field. It was a depressing moment for him. The stallion had carried him through four campaigns and had once been nursed by his devoted master through an attack of the strangles during five sleepless days and nights.

Alain had escaped more lightly. His sabre was intact and his horse, the valiant white which had been given to him by Emil, was cropping the grass contentedly, apparently oblivious to the gash in his flank.

As General Batut's aide Alain should not have been fighting at all, but had been given permission to do so when the general himself had been forced to retire from the field with an attack of asthma, a complaint to which he was subject.

'No sense in re-mounting,' Alain said, sliding down the trunk of the beech until his bottom touched the ground. The jar to his spine made him groan. 'It is almost over. The enemy are retreating in droves.'

'Another triumph for the Emperor,' said Emil. But victory had been dearly bought in a battle which had lasted for two whole days and had cost the French forty thousand casualties.

'I thought we were in for a drubbing

when that gap opened up in the centre,' Alain went on. 'The Imperial Guard plugged it just in time.'

'The Emperor's precious darlings are always just in time,' commented Emil sourly. 'One day they will be just too late.'

The July afternoon was hot and sultry, with the round disc of the sun hailing mankind from out of a cloudless sky, except in that small corner of Austria, where the great pall of smoke which hung over the battlefield obscured it completely. Four kilometres away in Vienna the people of that fine city waited and hoped to hear that their archduke, Charles, had won a great victory over the French usurper. As so often before, they were doomed to disappointment.

The two hussars, having taken a much needed breather, collected Alain's horse and mounting the patient animal, who showed no sign of resentment at the extra weight he was forced to bear upon his injured body, turned his head towards their base at the village of Aderklaa, half a kilometre to the south. All sounds of battle had ceased, but those other, more awful sounds, so familiar to seasoned soldiers, disturbed the uneasy stillness of the summer afternoon. They were the sounds of wounded and dying men groaning in their agony.

The riders gazed down upon the sprawled bodies, so undignified in death, and upon the writhing mass of mutilated humanity which moved among that fearful debris. They were filled with the usual sense of utter helplessness in face of the countless numbers requiring succour. Uniforms of every description met the eye, a crazy patchwork quilt of colourful carnage, which heaved and undulated as if spread across a gigantic green bed.

Alain and Emil were both compassionate men. It was always their custom after a battle to bring water to the wounded, although the search for this precious commodity was often long and wearying. Today was to be no exception. The terrain was unpromising and what streams and brooks there were were clogged with the filthy detritus of war which made the water unfit to drink. In the end the two were forced to dismount and pick their way among the dead in search of full water-bottles. Both collected as many as each could carry and set about the painstaking task of kneeling beside the wounded and pouring water into eagerly waiting mouths.

All over the battlefield other angels of mercy were similarly occupied, but crawling among them were also Satan's slime, the looters and murderers who turned up at the end of every battle to befoul the greatest sacrifice a man can make.

Alain came upon some men of his own regiment, several of whom, he was grieved to see, were quite beyond the puny aid he could offer. A trooper of dragoons stretched forth a beseeching hand. The gaping wound in his side had not in any way impaired his faculties and he asked through cracked lips, 'Sir, did we carry the day?'

Alain knelt down beside the man and removed the plug from a leather water-bottle. 'We did, trooper,' he replied. He supported the lolling head with his arm and placed the neck of the bottle to the parched lips. 'Slowly now. Do not gulp it down.'

Gently, he lowered the wounded man's head, remarking cheerfully as he did so, 'You will be taken up in a very short while by the flying ambulance and driven to the field hospital.'

The trooper's thanks were pathetically profuse and after giving him a friendly squeeze on the shoulder Alain passed on.

A prone figure, wearing the uniform of a hussar, obstructed his path. He thought the man was dead and was about to step over him when he heard a moan. A slight movement caught his eye. He bent down and turned the hussar over. A chilling scream rent the air and a deathly pale, pain-racked face streaked with blood and dirt, was disclosed to view. The eyelids of this corpse-like image flickered and parted and the blue eyes dawned with instant recognition.

'Alain!'

Alain had gone almost as pale as the wounded hussar. 'Christina? Is it you? My God, is it really you? What in heaven's name are you doing here?'

She tried unsuccessfully to smile. 'Dying, I think. I have a hole in my side.'

'Dear God, where?' He made as if to undo her jacket, but she pleaded with him not to touch her, adding pathetically, 'It hurts so much.'

'I must get you to the surgeon.'

Her head moved slowly from side to side and she gave a little whimper. 'It is no use. I am dying.'

'You cannot know that,' he argued desperately, and despite her repeated protests and cries of pain, he lifted her in his arms and began picking his way through the sea of bodies. Away to his right he could just see Emil, still intent on his mission of mercy and totally ignorant of his friend's astonishing discovery.

It took Alain twenty minutes to find his way to the field hospital with his burden. Christina had lapsed into unconsciousness and remained inert and silent during the jolting, uncomfortable progress.

Pasiello recognised him instantly and was less than helpful. 'It is you again, Captain,' he said testily. 'I wonder you did not take your friend straight to Surgeon Larrey, since you value his opinion more than mine.'

Having discharged himself of this satisfying witticism, Pasiello, like the good fellow he was, recalled himself to his duty. 'Put him down over there, if you please. I will attend to him in a little while.'

'I cannot.'

'Why? Has he got the plague?'

'No. *She* is seriously wounded.'

312

Pasiello's mouth actually dropped open. 'She? Did you say *she*?'

'Yes.'

'God have mercy. What is the world coming to when women invade the field of battle dressed as hussars? She wanted to be with her lover or her husband, I suppose. It is not completely unknown. Follow me, Captain.'

The hard-pressed man led Alain to a curtained-off corner of the massive tent, a small area of privacy where he kept his medical supplies and the camp-bed which he rarely had time to use. He pointed silently to the bed and Alain laid Christina upon it, after which he was requested to wait outside until the examination could be completed.

It seemed a long wait. Half an hour passed before he was recalled. Pasiello's first words were, 'Why did you not tell me it was Madame Batut? You must have recognised her. And what in hell is she doing going into battle? There will be the devil to pay when the general finds out.'

'Pasiello, will she live?' demanded Alain impatiently.

The other looked at him curiously. 'There is a slight chance she may survive. She has sustained a heavy flesh wound in her thigh and she has also suffered a miscarriage, which is not surprising under the circumstances. Perhaps Madame had a lover? Women do foolish things when they are in love.'

A hard look was directed at Alain, who stared straight back at the Italian without revealing any of his thoughts. He said, 'Perhaps it would be kinder to keep the general in ignorance of this strange affair until the outcome is more certain.'

Pasiello gave a non-committal grunt. 'I do not know about that. I would be sticking my neck out if the old man discovered I had treated his wife without letting him know.'

He passed a hand across his face, a gesture betokening both weariness and surrender. 'On the other hand, I take you for a man of honour, Captain, and am inclined to leave the whole matter to your discretion. I have too much to do to get myself tangled up in other people's private lives, although I would give much to know who scratched Madame's face before she decided to try her hand at the sword.' He gave a brittle laugh. 'Perhaps she had been fighting a duel.'

Alain digested the information about the scratch but paid it scant attention. 'Madame Batut cannot stay here,' he said. 'I will take her to a house in the village down the road and make arrangements for her to be looked after. If I let you know where she is, can you come in and see her once a day until she is recovered?'

Pasiello nodded briefly. 'I will do my best. I have applied what remedies I can and she is all bandaged up, but you had better take her some laudanum to deaden the pain. The rest we must leave to nature.'

The following day Alain visited Christina and sat by her bedside in the cottage of a cowman. The cowman had been well paid for his act of charity, but he was still scornful of the *putain*, as he referred to his unwelcome guest in the presence of his wife. He went on to express his disdain of camp followers who met their just deserts when they interfered in men's business.

The cowman's wife was less critical of the foreigner with the dark hair and the sad eyes. It was her opinion that 'the poor thing probably risked her life to drag her man off the field when he was wounded.'

'Dressed in a soldier's uniform?' sneered her husband.

'For decency's sake,' she insisted.

'Well, I hope she can move on soon,' came the unsympathetic rejoinder. 'She is an enemy when all is said and done.'

For almost twenty-four hours Christina lay on her back, unmoving and uncommunicative, and it was only when Alain came to see her that she opened her eyes and stirred into life. As he sat down beside her she offered him her hand. He took it between his own. 'You will be moving on soon, I expect?' she said.

'In a couple of days,' he confirmed. 'The regiment will not move on until the necessary repairs to wagons and limbers have been carried out.'

'Marie-Josèphe will be glad to see you safe and sound.'

'I have no doubt of it.'

'There is something I must tell you, Alain.'

'Not now. When you feel stronger.'

'No, now,' she insisted. 'Prop me up a little, will you?'

He let go of her hand and putting his arm around her, eased her up so that her head and shoulders were slightly raised against the two pillows which the cowman's wife had generously provided from her marriage-chest.

Christina stifled the cry of pain which rose from her throat and emerged through her lips only as a faint moan. Again her hand reached out for his and again he took it. The silence stretched between them. Alain felt as if he stood on the brink of eternity.

When at last she broke the silence Christina's voice seemed stronger as she launched into an account of the events which had taken place between herself and Marie-Josèphe at Stuttgart. It was as though she had been hoarding all her meagre reserves of energy for this moment when she must open her heart to the man she loved.

As the strange tale unfolded, Alain's astonishment grew and with it a feeling of anger that he had, albeit unwittingly, become a bone of contention between those whom he had sincerely loved. His head, bent over in a listening attitude, presented to Christina a profile both serious and troubled. She sensed the anger lurking behind the severity of his expression and understood the reason for it.

She said softly, 'It was your misfortune to be caught between two determined women, Alain, one of whom must now loose her hold upon you.'

He made no comment on this observation, asking instead, 'Did Marie-Josèphe really threaten to leave me and take away my children?'

'Yes.'

'Then her professions of love for me are false.'

'That is unfair. She loves you deeply.'

'And you? Do you love me deeply?'

'You know I do, but you will have to let me go, Alain.'

'Where will you go?'

'Perhaps I shall join my dead comrades-in-arms, wherever they are now.'

'You are not going to die.'

'I think so.'

'Surgeon Pasiello says you are holding your own.'

'Pasiello does not know how I feel inside. One senses these things.'

'So-called feminine intuition can often lead one astray. You are simply feeling depressed.'

In an effort to shake her out of her fatalistic mood he broached a subject she had not yet touched on in detail. 'You have not told me how you managed to join the army.'

He saw that she was uncomfortable and rearranged her pillows. She rewarded him with a strained smile. 'I did not, at least not in the way you mean. I simply bought myself a uniform, a sabre and a horse, passing off all these items as gifts for a non-existent nephew, and infiltrated myself into Marshal Massena's corps. It was not difficult in the confusion before a battle. I had to pin up my hair, of course.'

The painful smile dissolved. 'Alain, will you promise me something?'

'If what you are about to ask of me is within my power to accomplish.'

'When I die, will you see that I am

buried here, with the men. I am, after all, a soldier's woman.'

He shook his head. 'You are not going to die, Christina.'

Her eyes had the patient look of a mother dealing with a difficult child. 'Will you promise if I concede that we are merely discussing a possibility?'

He nodded reluctantly.

'There is one more thing.'

'Yes?'

'If the worst should happen, will you break the news to my husband?' Her eyes held his. 'And tell him that I indulged a whim to become a cavalryman. He will understand why. He may even applaud my daring, especially when he knows that I killed two of the enemy before I was myself unhorsed.'

Gently, she teased him. 'Have you nothing to say? Come now, I cannot believe that I have provoked you to envy.'

His head was bent over her hand, which he was stroking in a slow and tender caress, that slender white hand which had held the death-dealing sabre. There were tears in his eyes. He said, 'The child you were carrying, was it mine?'

Her face changed. 'So Pasiello told you. You should not have asked me that. What does it matter now whose child it was?'

'No, I am sorry. I should not have asked.'

'Go home to Marie-Josèphe, Alain. Go home now.'

'I cannot leave you like this.'

She gave a little sigh and closed her eyes. 'I am so very tired.'

He bent to kiss her cheek and her eyes flew open. 'Do not be angry with me, Alain, or with Marie-Josèphe because of what we have done.'

A small defeated sigh escaped him. 'You spoke to me of a wife I did not recognise. I had never imagined her to be capable of such a thing, or that you could be a party to it. Were you so uncertain of my love that you thought a mark on your face would banish it for ever?'

'You admire only beautiful women, Alain.'

'To me, *you* are beautiful. And do you think me so facile a man that a blemish will turn admiration into disgust?'

She put up her hand and fingered the scar on her face.

'Vanity is a fearful taskmaster. But it was not only that. There was a moment when we were duelling that I looked at Marie-Josèphe's face and knew, without a shadow of doubt, that she wanted to kill me. It was only for a moment, but when I saw her expression I realised that what we were doing, you and I, was wrong. We were destroying another person's life. I felt ashamed then and later, when I received the wound, I thought, this is my punishment for what I have done.'

'Precious nonsense!' he muttered crossly.

'Maybe, but the fact remains that you have a tigress for a wife, Alain, and a fool for a mistress. It is time for you to tame the tigress and dispense with the fool. Go home, please go home as soon as you can.'

Christina closed her eyes again, blotting out the concerned face of her lover, blotting out the world with which she had nothing more to do.

He stayed beside her until he was sure that she had fallen asleep, then released her hand and tiptoed away. At the door he turned once more to look at her. 'I shall come and see you tomorrow, soldier's woman.'

* * *

Early the following morning Pasiello went in search of Alain, leaving the field hospital to ride out to the open field where the 7th Hussars had set up their bivouac. The gravity of his expression betrayed the nature of his news.

'Madame Batut died during the night, Captain. I have had her body removed and placed before the altar in the village church. Please accept my condolences. I know you had a special interest in her.'

Pasiello was a liberal man, who questioned not the morals of his fellow human-beings. All the same, Alain's response, spoken in a tone of trance-like disbelief, embarrassed him.

'How could she leave me like that? We were lovers.'

Pasiello coughed and murmured, 'Yes, well, we had better not think of that just now,' a remark which seemed to bring the other to his senses. His eyes came back into focus and his body straightened as he offered an immediate apology.

'Forgive me. That was an appalling indiscretion. I will ride over to head-quarters this morning and inform General Batut of the tragedy.'

'I think we agreed that it would be better to allow him to think that his wife's body was discovered on the field.'

'Yes.'

Pasiello scratched his nose. 'We two are the only parties to the secret, I suppose, apart from the peasants who gave her shelter, and they don't signify?'

'My friend, Captain Durand, knows, but we have absolutely nothing to fear from that quarter.'

'No, I daresay not. You and Durand could not be closer if you were brothers. I will leave the matter in your hands then, Captain.' Pasiello gave a shake of the head which expressed both sorrow and disapproval. 'Devilish odd business all round, though. Whatever possessed her to do such a thing?'

Alain offered no enlightenment on this score and Pasiello shrugged off the matter with the comment that women often did strange things when they were breeding and that he had known one who had gone off her head altogether.

He had turned to go when he

suddenly remembered something and fumbling in the pocket of his rather shabby jacket, produced a crumpled letter and a locket, both of which he handed to Alain. 'I almost forgot. I found these under Madame Batut's pillow. The letter is addressed to you. Madame must have written it before she came to grief. If it contains material of an intimate nature you may thank God that it did not fall into the wrong hands.'

With that Pasiello stomped off, acknowledging with a wave of his hand the other's expressions of gratitude.

Alain stuffed both letter and locket into the pocket at the front of his breeches. To read the letter now, whatever its contents, would cause him too much pain. He went for a walk, bending his head against a stiff breeze. His sense of desolation surpassed anything he would ever have thought possible.

* * *

Alain ran General Batut to earth at the Emperor's headquarters at Kaiser-Ebersdorf and broke the news of his wife's death, offering his condolences in a voice which conveyed nothing of his own feelings. At the sight of his wife's locket resting in the palm of Alain's hand the general broke down and wept. Alain looked away until the bereaved man had sufficiently recovered his composure to say, 'I told you she should have been a man, didn't I? Suppose she wanted to know what it felt like to carry a sword into battle.'

He gave a choking sort of laugh which disintegrated into a distressing wheeze. 'One thing is certain. She could not have done it for love of the Emperor. Expressed her views pretty forcibly on the subject of our Corsican friend. Always had the fear she might forget herself one day and do it in public.'

The general suddenly seemed to recollect that this was no occasion for mirth and wiped his damp face with an enormous red handkerchief which he drew from his pocket like a conjurer producing a flag. 'You found her, you say, Captain?'

'Yes, sir, while I was taking water to the wounded.'

'And she was dead?'

'Yes, sir.'

'Where is she now?'

Alain told him.

The general thanked his aide for what he had done and declared his intention of taking his wife's body back to Strasbourg for burial. Alain hesitated. In his mind's eye he saw Christina's pale face and pleading blue eyes. 'Promise me, Alain . . . promise.'

He said, 'If you will forgive the presumption on my part, sir, I think Madame Batut would have wanted to be buried on the field with the men.'

A pleased look crossed the general's face. 'Do you, Captain? By heaven, I think you are right.'

The single eye bolted itself to Alain's face. 'She *was* really dead when you found her? Not trying to spare my feelings?'

'Madame Batut was dead, sir,' replied Alain firmly.

The eye was disconcertingly steady. 'Clever of you, Captain, to guess she would want to lie with the fallen. Almost as if you had heard the request from her own lips.'

Alain remained prudently silent and prayed that curiosity would not harden into suspicion. To his relief the eye wavered and released him. 'Thought she had gone to Stuttgart to enjoy herself . . . theatres, balls, shooting-parties, that sort of thing. Had no idea what was in her mind. Would not have let her come if I had. That goes without saying, of course.'

Alain felt very sorry for the general, who was talking now for the sake of talking, holding his grief at bay. He came to his rescue by offering to accompany him to the field funeral of his wife.

The eye was concentrated once more.

'Good of you, Captain. Appreciate the gesture. Fitting really. You once had an interest.'

'*I know you had a special interest.*' Was not that what Pasiello had said? An interest. It was a strange, business-like sort of word to describe what he had felt about Christina.

She was buried the next day, a day of rain and moaning wind which swept across the bleak field of death and stirred the tattered debris of battle. Christina lay as she had wished, among the fallen, her comrades-in-arms, and the ritual words were said over the plain pinewood coffin by the regimental chaplain. The chaplain moved on, unsurprised that he had committed to the ground a woman, one Christina Calvi he had been told. She was probably only a soldier's woman.

Alain moved away too and left the general to mourn his wife alone. The two men who had borne the coffin from the village church to the field were hovering expectantly nearby. Alain fumbled in the pocket of his breeches and brought out some coins which he offered with a brief word of thanks for the service they had rendered. His hand returned to his pocket, where it had come into contact with a folded piece of paper. Christina's letter. He had forgotten all about it, so preoccupied had he been with seeing the general and attending the funeral. He glanced over his shoulder. The widower was still keeping vigil beside the gaping hole which had received his late wife's remains. A little way away two soldiers leant on their shovels as they waited to fill in the hole and wondered why the general seemed so concerned about the death of a female camp follower.

Alain turned his back on the depressing scene and unfolded the single sheet of paper. Her bold hand-writing leapt up at him, reminding him poignantly of the shopping lists she used to write out every day when they lived together at the house of Madame La Harpe, and about which he had teased her unmercifully, saying that if she could not carry two or three items in her head without writing them down she would never make a good housewife. He fought back a rush of emotion as her opening words clawed at his grief:-

'My dearest Alain, If you read this letter I shall be dead, for it cannot come into your possession in any other way. By now you will know what I have done. I am tempted to say that I did it for you, but that will only make you angry and anyway it is not the truth. I have done what I have done for purely selfish reasons. I could not bear you to see me as I am now, with a scar on my face. (How I came to be scarred is of no consequence).

'So now you know why I wanted to die in battle. I am very much afraid, as I prepare to make my grand gesture, but you always used to say that a soldier who says he is not afraid when he goes into battle is either a fool or a liar. I have been both in my time. It was foolish of me to fall in love with a man I could never really call my own and even more foolish to persist in my attachment to him when the game was well and truly lost.

'As to the other deadly sin, I only ever lied to you once, Alain, and that was in regard to my family. My father was not a magistrate, a fact which I believe you suspected. His work commenced only after the magistrate had pronounced sentence of death upon some poor wretch. He was the public executioner.

'Our family, my mother, father and myself, lived in a small house right in the middle of a field in a village just outside Turin. We lived apart from the other villagers because none of them wanted to have anything to do with us. As you may imagine, I was a very lonely child and always I carried with me a feeling of deep shame that I was the daughter of such a man. Coupled with the shame was an even deeper guilt that I did not love my father as a dutiful child should.

'During the Terror my father was often called upon to go to France, to Lyon mainly, to help despatch the aristocrats who had offended the government. He used to bring back with him all manner of trinkets — rings, necklaces, bracelets, watches, miniatures, set in gold and encircled with diamonds — and these he would sell, sometimes travelling as far afield as southern Spain for the purpose. The trinkets were freely given to him by the condemned as part of his recognised fee. He never stole anything. As a child I would look at the jewellery curiously and with childish greed long to possess a bracelet or a necklace which I thought particularly beautiful, but my father never allowed my mother and me to do much more than look and later, when I came to realise what these pretty things represented, the last and most precious possessions of those doomed to die, the sight of them repelled me and I would turn my head away when my father tipped them out from his leather bag on to our kitchen table.

'Despite this repugnance on my part, however, there was one occasion when my eye was attracted by a locket which bounced off the table on to the floor and sprang open of its own accord to reveal the miniature of a lady. As I bent to retrieve the locket, curiosity overcame revulsion and I examined the portrait with some attention. It was of a fair-haired, grey-eyed lady and I think the artist had captured with his brush something of her character. So calm and lovely she looked, with the suggestion of a smile hovering about her lips.

'If only, I thought, as I gazed at the pale, composed features, this had been my mother! Need I say that even as the thought took root, guilt forced its way uppermost in my mind that my own mother meant so little to me? Selfishly, I had never stopped to think that my father's occupation had made her the morose, irritable creature she was.

'Almost before I knew what I was about I had slipped the locket into the bosom of my dress, aware as I did so that my father was studying with particular interest a most elegant gentleman's timepiece in a turquoise-studded case. To my relief he did not notice the absence of the locket — his haul was considerable that day — and even if he had I would not have owned up to stealing it, for I had found something on which to build a dream.

'From that time on the lady in the miniature became my true mother and I wove about her a fantasy that I had been stolen from her as a child and adopted by these strange and fearful people who called themselves my parents. When they died of the plague I felt little sorrow at their passing. Now my dream could become reality. I could wear the locket on its gold chain about my neck and I would tell anyone who cared to ask that it contained the portrait of my mother. I would leave my village and make a life for myself, become like other people at last, respectable and respected.

'Even as I write these words I feel ashamed. I showed you the lady in the miniature, Alain, and told you she was my mother. You thought her very beautiful and I was pleased. I should have been sickened by the deception I was practising upon you, for could not that locket have been the last precious possession of your father? You will say no, never in a million years would your father have given into the hands of the common executioner the image of the wife he loved so dearly. But who knows what a man so near to death will do if his mind is in a state of confusion? What if it had been your mother's portrait which I wore about my neck? Would you not have killed me in an agony of rage and pain to see it so besmirched?

'Now that you know the guilty secrets of my heart, Alain, I hope you will still cherish the memory of one who loved you dearly. My husband, poor deluded creature, knows nothing of my origins, only that I was once a soldier's woman. He married me in spite of that and I could not bring myself to heap further humiliation upon him by telling him that he had also married the daughter of a hangman. You see, I wanted respectability so much that I was willing to lie and cheat to get it. But you saw through me, Alain. You always saw through me. Good-bye, my darling. Your soldier's woman.'

Alain re-folded the letter and put it back in his pocket. His face felt wet and he wiped it on the sleeve of his jacket. He had never felt so sorry for any human being in the whole of his life. To live with a tortured conscience must be fearful indeed. It occurred to him that if Christina had been dead when he found her he might never have known about the duel. Would Marie-Josèphe have told him the sorry tale, or would she too have become the unwilling possessor of a shameful secret? Do not think about it he adjured himself and was seized by a sudden and most urgent longing to hold his children in his arms.

The general was walking towards him with his shoulders hunched forward and his sombre, intent gaze fixed upon the ground. Expressions of sympathy, thought Alain, had gone far enough. It was time to allow practicalities to take over. As soon as the bent figure came within hearing distance he offered,

'Shall I ride back to Kaiser-Ebersdorf with you, sir?'

The answer was gruff and to the point. 'Don't need a nursemaid, I thank you, Captain. If you are feeling helpful, though, you could rout about and find me a new horse. I think my poor old brute has got glanders. Shan't shoot him. He don't deserve that. Take him home and put him out to grass. Come to think of it, it might be high time I put myself out to grass. What is your opinion?'

Alain hid a smile and replied truthfully, 'I think you have a good few battles left in you yet, sir.'

'Do you, by God? That is a very pretty compliment, Captain. And now you have done with licking my boots, go and find me that horse, there's a good fellow.'

14

Strasbourg
August, 1809

The Café Violette was crowded. Two hussars, shakos tucked confidently under their arms, pushed their way through the press of people and occupied their favourite corner table. The waiter brought them two cognacs.

'A full house tonight,' said one, looking about him.

'Unblooded youth,' replied his companion contemptuously. 'Not a hair out of place.'

'Do I detect a note of cynicism, a hint of battle weariness, a soupçon of envy for the bright, untarnished youth of France?'

Captain Alain d'Albert laughed. 'You do, my friend, you do. I cannot stand the sight of these fancy fellows straight out of the Academy.'

'Have a heart. The only danger the poor wretches present is to unattached women. The enemy certainly have nothing to fear from them because the powers-that-be no longer teach them to survive. I doubt if they will wear as well as we have.'

Captain Emil Durand tipped back his cognac. '*Salut*! This reminds me of old times. How long is it since we came to the Café Violette?'

Alain considered the question. 'It must be at least four years since our shadows darkened the doors of this unpretentious establishment, which I observe still attracts all the unmarried bucks. Sober military men like ourselves have no business here.'

'Speak for yourself. I am still in my green and carefree days.'

'Your green and carefree days are turning a bit brown round the edges, my friend. You should have married Elise before she got tired of waiting for you to make up your mind and dragged that drunken sergeant of dragoons to the altar.'

Emil chuckled. 'I have it on the best authority that the sergeant has become sober as a judge now that his new wife has taken him in hand.'

'Well, at least you seem to have recovered your spirits. I remember you were like a bear with a sore head when Elise ran off.'

'I loved the silly bitch, but I could never make her understand that a binding contract would shatter our relationship to pieces. We should have been at each other's throats in a week. She would not have it, though. Women can be so irrational when they have determined upon trapping a man for good.'

Alain pulled a face, drained his glass and signalled to the waiter to bring two more cognacs. 'You are telling *me*?'

Emil, who was feeling very convivial, did his best to look serious. 'Have you forgiven Marie-Josèphe for playing the man?'

'Surely you mean playing the fool? The trouble with women is that besides being irrational they never think things through. They dream up some completely impractical idea and pursue it to its conclusion, regardless of the fact that the way is strewn with thorns, any one of which should be enough to stop them in their tracks. Now we have a situation where I feel guilty, my wife feels guilty and between us we have erected a barrier which will take some breaking down. In time, of course, it will fall, because no one can go on feeling guilty for ever. Guilt is a physical thing. It drains away one's energy.'

'None of it was your fault,' Emil said.

'Oh, but it was. I should have realised that Marie-Josèphe was a woman who could not stand female competition.'

'There are a lot of women like that. They do not all challenge their rivals to duels. They sit at home minding their children and pretending that the rival does not exist.'

'Is that how you think a wife should behave?'

'Certainly I do.'

Alain toyed with his second cognac. 'I am not sure that I agree with you. I like a woman with spirit. A complacent woman resembles a blancmange, all soft and tasteless.' He sighed deeply. 'If only one could start all over again, wipe the slate clean. The hell of it is that Marie-Josèphe simply wanted to frighten Christina off, not drive her to commit suicide.'

'You have chewed it over long enough, don't you think? It would be better now to try and forget it.'

The two friends exchanged glances, with concern on one side and amusement on the other.

Alain declared with conviction, 'I am becoming a bore.'

'Only now and then, old fellow.'

'Enough said. I must put paid to that nonsense at once. Do you see that pretty girl over there in the red dress with the flowers in her hair? She is looking at you as if she would like to swallow you whole.'

Emil grinned and stood up. 'Perhaps I ought to let her then? If you will excuse me, Captain?'

Alain waved a magnanimous hand. 'Take as long as you like.'

Five minutes later, however, Emil was back and ordering another cognac. Alain looked up in surprise from his third glass of that inspiriting substance. 'Now do not tell me that the old magic has ceased to work?' His face split into a grin. 'Come to think of it, you are sprouting a few grey hairs here and there. Perhaps you remind the young lady too much of her father.'

Emil sat down with a sheepish smile spreading across his face. 'To tell you the truth, old fellow, I think she would have made a most agreeable replacement for Elise, but . . . '

'But what?' demanded Alain impatiently as the other groped for words.

Emil, obviously embarrassed, struggled to explain himself. 'You know how on the night before a battle I turn my jacket inside out and tie a red ribbon to my horse's bridle?'

'Because you are a superstitious old Gascon, yes?'

'Yes.'

'Well for heaven's sake what has that got to do with taking another woman?'

Emil avoided Alain's eyes, coughed discreetly and murmured, 'She told me her name was Christina.' '

THE END

Other titles in the Linford Romance Library

SAVAGE PARADISE
Sheila Belshaw

For four years, Diana Hamilton had dreamed of returning to Luangwa Valley in Zambia. Now she was back — and, after a close encounter with a rhino — was receiving a lecture from a tall, khaki-clad man on the dangers of going into the bush alone!

PAST BETRAYALS
Giulia Gray

As soon as Jon realized that Julia had fallen in love with him, he broke off their relationship and returned to work in the Middle East. When Jon's best friend, Danny, proposed a marriage of friendship, Julia accepted. Then Jon returned and Julia discovered her love for him remained unchanged.

PRETTY MAIDS ALL IN A ROW
Rose Meadows

The six beautiful daughters of George III of England dreamt of handsome princes coming to claim them, but the King always found some excuse to reject proposals of marriage. This is the story of what befell the Princesses as they began to seek lovers at their father's court, leaving behind rumours of secret marriages and illegitimate children.

THE GOLDEN GIRL
Paula Lindsay

Sarah had everything — wealth, social background, great beauty and magnetic charm. Her heart was ruled by love and compassion for the less fortunate in life. Yet, when one man's happiness was at stake, she failed him — and herself.

A DREAM OF HER OWN
Barbara Best

A stranger gently kisses Sarah Danbury at her Betrothal Ball. Little does she realise that she is to meet this mysterious man again in very different circumstances.

HOSTAGE OF LOVE
Nara Lake

From the moment pretty Emma Tregear, the only child of a Van Diemen's Land magnate, met Philip Despard, she was desperately in love. Unfortunately, handsome Philip was a convict on parole.

THE ROAD TO BENDOUR
Joyce Eaglestone

Mary Mackenzie had lived a sheltered life on the family farm in Scotland. When she took a job in the city she was soon in a romantic maze from which only she could find the way out.

NEW BEGINNINGS
Ann Jennings

On the plane to his new job in a hospital in Turkey, Felix asked Harriet to put their engagement on hold, as Philippe Krir, the Director of Bodrum hospital, refused to hire 'attached' people. But, without an engagement ring, what possible excuse did Harriet have for holding Philippe at bay?

THE CAPTAIN'S LADY
Rachelle Edwards

1820: When Lianne Vernon becomes governess at Elswick Manor, she finds her young pupil is given to strange imaginings and that her employer, Captain Gideon Lang, is the most enigmatic man she has ever encountered. Soon Lianne begins to fear for her pupil's safety.

THE VAUGHAN PRIDE
Margaret Miles

As the new owner of Southwood Manor, Laura Vaughan discovers that she's even more poverty stricken than before. She also finds that her neighbour, the handsome Marius Kerr, is a little too close for comfort.

HONEY-POT
Mira Stables

Lovely, well-born, well-dowered, Russet Ingram drew all men to her. Yet here she was, a prisoner of the one man immune to her graces — accused of frivolously tampering with his young ward's romance!

DREAM OF LOVE
Helen McCabe

When there is a break-in at the art gallery she runs, Jade can't believe that Corin Bossinney is a trickster, or that she'd fallen for the oldest trick in the book . . .

FOR LOVE OF OLIVER
Diney Delancey

When Oliver Scott buys her family home, Carly retains the stable block from which she runs her riding school. But she soon discovers Oliver is not an easy neighbour to have. Then Carly is presented with a new challenge, one she must face for love of Oliver.

THE SECRET OF MONKS' HOUSE
Rachelle Edwards

Soon after her arrival at Monks' House, Lilith had been told that it was haunted by a monk, and she had laughed. Of greater interest was their neighbour, the mysterious Fabian Delamaye. Was he truly as debauched as rumour told, and what was the truth about his wife's death?

THE SPANISH HOUSE
Nancy John

Lynn couldn't help falling in love with the arrogant Brett Sackville. But Brett refused to believe that she felt nothing for his half-brother, Rafael. Lynn knew that the cruel game Brett made her play to protect Rafael's heart could end only by breaking hers.

PROUD SURGEON
Lynne Collins

Calder Savage, the new Senior Surgical Officer at St. Antony's Hospital, had really lived up to his name, venting a savage irony on anyone who fell foul of him. But when he gave Staff Nurse Honor Portland a lift home, she was surprised to find what an interesting man he was.

A PARTNER FOR PENNY
Pamela Forest

Penny had grown up with Christopher Lloyd and saw in him the older brother she'd never had. She was dismayed when he was arrogantly confident that she should not trust her new business colleague, Gerald Hart. She opposed Chris by setting out to win Gerald as a partner both in love and business.

SURGEON ASHORE
Ann Jennings

Luke Roderick, the new Consultant Surgeon for Accident and Emergency, couldn't understand why Staff Nurse Naomi Selbourne refused to apply for the vacant post of Sister. Naomi wasn't about to tell him that she moonlighted as a waitress in order to support her small nephew, Toby.

A MOONLIGHT MEETING
Peggy Gaddis

Megan seemed to have fallen under handsome Tom Fallon's spell, and she was no longer sure if she would be happy as Larry's wife. It was only in the aftermath of a terrible tragedy that she realized the true meaning of love.

THE STARLIT GARDEN
Patricia Hemstock

When interior designer Tansy Donaghue accepted a commission to restore Beechwood Manor in Devon, she was relieved to leave London and its memories of her broken romance with architect Robert Jarvis. But her dream of a peaceful break was shattered not only by Robert's unexpected visit, but also by the manipulative charms of the manor's owner, James Buchanan.

THE BECKONING DAWN
Georgina Ferrand

For twenty-five years Caroline has lived the life of a recluse, believing she is ugly because of a facial scar. After a successful operation, the handsome Anton Tessler comes into her life. However, Caroline soon learns that the kind of love she yearns for may never be hers.

THE WAY OF THE HEART
Rebecca Marsh

It was the scandal of the season when world-famous actress Andrea Lawrence stalked out of a Broadway hit to go home again. But she hadn't jeopardized her career for nothing. The beautiful star was onstage for the play of her life — a drama of double-dealing romance starring her sister's fiancé.

VIENNA MASQUERADE
Lorna McKenzie

In Austria, Kristal Hastings meets Rodolfo von Steinberg, the young cousin of Baron Gustav von Steinberg, who had been her grandmother's lover many years ago. An instant attraction flares between them — but how can Kristal give her love to Rudi when he is already promised to another . . . ?

HIDDEN LOVE
Margaret McDonagh

Until his marriage, Matt had seemed like an older brother to Teresa. Now, five years later, Matt's wife has tragically died and Teresa feels she must go and comfort him. But how much longer can she hold on to the secret that has been hers for all these years?

A MOST UNUSUAL MARRIAGE
Barbara Best

Practically penniless, Dorcas Wareham meets Suzette, who tells her that she had rashly married a Captain Jack Bickley on the eve of his leaving for the Boer War. She suggests that Dorcas takes her place, saying that Jack didn't expect to survive the war anyway. With some misgivings, Dorcas finally agrees. But Jack does return . . .

A TOUCH OF TENDERNESS
Juliet Gray

Ben knew just how to charm, how to captivate a woman — though he could not win a heart that was already in another man's keeping. But Clare was desperately anxious to protect him from a pain she knew too well herself.

NEED FOR A NURSE
Lynne Collins

When Kelvin, a celebrated actor, regained consciousness after a car accident, he had lost his memory. He was shocked to learn that he was engaged to the beautiful actress Beth Hastings. His mind was troubled — and so was his heart when he became aware of the impact on his emotions of a pretty staff nurse . . .

WHISPER OF DOUBT
Rachel Croft

Fiona goes to Culvie Castle to value paintings for the owner, who is in America. After meeting Ewen McDermott, the heir to the castle, Fiona suspects that there is something suspicious going on. But little does she realise what heartache lies ahead of her . . .

MISTRESS AT THE HALL
Eileen Knowles

Sir Richard Thornton makes Gina welcome at the Hall, but his grandson, Zachary, calls her a fortune hunter. After Sir Richard's death, Gina finds taking over the role of Mistress at the Hall far from easy, and Zachary doesn't help — until he realises that he loves her.

PADLOCK YOUR HEART
Anne Saunders

Ignoring James Thornton's warning that it was cruel to give false hope, Faith set up a fund to send little Debby to Russia for treatment. Despite herself, Faith found she was falling in love with James. Perhaps she should have padlocked her heart against him.